Georgia, A New York Story

By Carol Lucha-Burns

Georgia, A New York Story

Copyright and Publisher

Georgia, A New York Story

A Lucha-Burns, LLC Book

ISBN: 0988295728
ISBN – 13: 978-0-9882957-2-8

First published in 2012
Revision 3 Published March 2013

Lucha-Burns, LLC
PO Box 10
Whitefield, NH 03598-0010
United States of America

Cover by Robert C. Gault
Photo by Perry A. Smith

Printed in the United States of America

Thanks and Dedication

Heart-felt thanks to my 'eclectic family'. Your continuing love makes me realize how fortunate we are to be connected by choice. Additional kudos to Brian, Ceil, Corbie, D. Michael, Deah, Donna, Erik, John, JWG, Laurel, Meg, Peggy, Peter, Rick, Scott and Sharon – it wouldn't have been as honest without you.

Dedicated to Meg and Joanna for starting me on the writing journey.

Table of Contents

Georgia, A New York Story

Foreword

For the past several years I have been after Georgia, my retired college professor mother to write our family history. Occasionally, she would e-mail delightful, tied-in-a-bow, happy ending stories about my grandparents, the foibles of her youth, and surprisingly, the loss of her virginity at age twenty-one. These anecdotal tales are funny and often poignant, but she later admitted she was using them to avoid writing her memoirs. If someone needed her she reveled in what she referred to as another 'teachable moment' and off she would go on a new project that allowed her continuing procrastination.

On Christmas of 2011, at age 70, several months after the tenth anniversary of what we refer to as 9/11, she told me she was ready to write our unique family history, but not until she completed a novel based on the most important six months in our lives. This is that book.

Val Shultze-Hogan, Summer 2012

MOM'S FAVORITE QUOTES

"Today is the Tomorrow You Worried About Yesterday…"——Dale Carnegie

There are more horses asses in the world than horses."——Rudy Shultze

Chapter 1

Where Do People Go?

Kelly Christine Thompson stood on the shoulder of the busy Baltimore Pike in the relentless downpour, her thumb extended. She considered throwing herself into the path of a passing truck and ending the emotional and physical pain of the past month. In this cloudburst, she wouldn't be seen. And besides, the roads were too slick to stop in time, even if she was spotted. Anything would be better than Kennett Square, Pennsylvania and...Barry. Wearing nothing but soaked jeans and a cotton shirt that clung to her shivering body she was almost hit by a green Subaru wagon that skidded to a stop. A young woman's head emerged from the passenger window, "Hurry in, you're drenched." Kelly jumped in the back to the dry warmth of the car. Two faces, a girl in her early twenties and a middle-aged, slightly balding, dark-haired male driver, greeted her.

The pretty blonde turned to face her. "Hi, I'm Val." She prattled on. "My driver friend Ricky and I are on our way back to New York." Kelly couldn't stop shivering from a mixture of fear and cold. Val tossed her a Diesel hooded sweatshirt. "Here put this on. Where are you heading?"

Kelly lied, "I'm on my way to New York to look at colleges."

They crossed the Delaware Memorial Bridge into New Jersey. Kelly felt safer. She was one state further away from Barry.

Val was elated, "We're driving to Tenth Avenue and 22nd Street but we can drop you anywhere in Manhattan. By the way, what's your name?"

Determined to escape her past Kelly created a name based on her initials, K.C. She spelled it out. "K–A–S–E–Y." She said it at a faster pace, "Kasey, Kasey Thompson." It sounded believable and she began to doze as she embraced the warmth of the car. Two hours later, she awoke to a clear view of the New York skyline. The colored lights twinkled like stars fallen to earth. The city looked huge and better still, anonymous. At last she could be safe.

After an hour in the Lincoln Tunnel, they screeched to a halt on 22nd Street near Tenth Avenue. On the fence across the way was a sign that said Clement Clarke Moore Park. Kasey considered that it must be named for the poet who wrote *A Visit From St. Nicholas*. She smiled for the poem brought loving memories of her childhood before her father died and her mother remarried.

The reminiscence escaped as Val's driver opened the car door and held out his hand. Instinctively she pulled away from him and moved to Val, "Thank you for saving me."

Kasey handed her the hoodie. Val shook her head, "No, keep it. I'll borrow it back if I need it. Come and meet my mother." Val pulled Kasey toward her parents' single-family brick townhouse, "We live in the entire house, except for the one bedroom apartment on the fourth floor which we rent, at a nominal cost, to my driver friend Ricky. You'll move

3

in with us until you get settled."

"Oh, I couldn't, you've been too kind already."

Val scoffed, "Don't be silly. We've lots of room. Dad's consulting business takes him all over Asia so Mom runs the house and worries until we're all safe and sound at home. I'm surprised she isn't sitting on the stoop waiting." Just then, the doors opened and out popped a 60ish, tall, slender brunette, in paint-covered jeans, sporting an *I Love New York* T-shirt, and waving a dripping orange paintbrush.

Georgia rushed down the stairs, "I'm so relieved you're here." After hugging Val and Horace (who Val called Ricky), she noticed the hesitant stranger in Val's hoodie. "And who's this? Some homeless person you happened to pick up along the way? Or is she a runaway bride from that wedding?"

Val laughed. "Mom meet Kasey, a mysterious refugee we found hitching a ride outside Kennett Square, Pennsylvania. Kasey, meet Georgia. She needs a place to stay. Do you mind?"

"Not at all, we've plenty of room. I just finished painting the guest room bright orange. If I'd known you were coming, with that red hair, I would have chosen a vibrant green color for the walls. Did you know that Lucille Ball's dressing room was Emerald Green? Well, never mind, I'll put you in the floral wallpaper room. It's just as nice and you'll be closer to the bathroom."

Georgia took Kasey upstairs, saying, "We'd better get you out of those damp clothes and into something dry. You

4

must have been in a very big hurry to leave Pennsylvania. You forgot your suitcase."

Kasey realized that Georgia was more astute than her paint spattered clothes and scattered personality initially led one to believe. She blushed. "I can't thank you enough for taking me in. You don't even know me; I could be the Unabomber."

Georgia's blue eyes twinkled as she asked, "Where are you hiding the bomb? In that forgotten suitcase?" Kasey was embarrassed, but Georgia reassured her. "Don't worry. John and I trust people until they prove otherwise. We have very few rules in this house, which is why you will see people coming and going at will. We have a combination lock that allows access to those we trust. We share what we have. Friends in the neighborhood often use our library. Some you may find raiding the larder, but the food is replaced the next time the welfare check arrives."

"But how will I know who to let in?"

"You aren't here as a servant, you're here as a member of the family. People we cherish have the combination to the outside door and we have never had it changed. You'll notice the door to your room and bathroom have inside locks so you should feel safe and now I'll say goodnight."

"The rules?"

"Oh, yes. Thoughts whir in and out of my head so quickly I often start something and go off on a tangent. Our one rule requires absolute honesty. We will not condone liars, and in John's and my world, a lie is the intent to deceive."

Examining Kasey's face, Georgia elaborated, "That being said, everyone is entitled to their secrets and their privacy. You're safe here. Trust me, my little runaway, when you are ready to confide you will. And now, goodnight and sleep tight." She winked as she closed the door.

Chapter 2

Food Glorious Food

Horace parked the Subaru and hurried to his one-bedroom apartment on the fourth floor. As his HP portable laptop booted up he reflected on his mother's anger when his six-month marriage ended in divorce four years ago. For forty-eight months she had harangued him for not having a wife, which is why he was excited about his burgeoning online relationship with a girl who found him on the Internet.

He was so desperate to be involved with someone that he hid his disappointment at not hearing the familiar "You've got mail" and forged ahead with his tedious two finger typing. He spent the next four hours thinking, typing, reading, analyzing, deleting, composing, reading, deleting, rubbing his head and worrying. As dawn broke, satisfied with his three sentences, he hit send. It was four in the morning.

Twelve hours later Horace headed for the Village to meet his drinking buddies. This was a weekly event but today he found the banter boring and left feeling quite despondent. It was raining. As usual, he forgot his umbrella and since he refused to wear a hat he returned home quite wet and miserable.

Val spent part of the day showing Kasey the neighborhood. They arrived home with two pizzas, hung up their wet slickers and slipped off their sodden sneakers in an attempt to keep the parquet floors from getting water stained.

7

Georgia was usually casual about the items in their art-laden home, but since she and John (her do-it-yourself husband of thirty years) had hand restored the multi-directional squares of wooden flooring, she insisted that they retain a showcase quality.

A tipsy Horace followed them in. He shook himself like a wet cocker spaniel and sprayed water all over the floor. Georgia yelled, "Horace, stop that!"

He scampered to the kitchen and returned with paper towels to dry his hair and the floor. "Sorry, it is pouring out there."

Val wrinkled her nose at him as she set the table. "It's easy to smell you've been with your drinking buddies at your favorite watering hole." She checked the kitchen clock. "Usually you're out until 10:00. What happened?"

"Today the bar depressed me. Tonight, for the first time, I realized that I do not belong. Not there. Not anywhere."

Val attempted to lift him from his usual Sunday night depression. "Ricky, you belong here and you know it. After all, we've put up with your swinging moods for nearly three years. You're Mom's newest project. Until you're fine-tuned, she won't give up on you."

She began singing, "Nobody likes me. Everybody hates me! I'm gonna eat some worms."

Georgia interrupted, "What kind of pizza did you girls get? Smells good."

8

"Pepperoni and, I hope you don't mind, Hawaiian, Kasey's favorite."

An appalled Horace sniffed in haughty disgust. "Authentic pizza has sausage, and vegetables." Val, refusing to let his disgruntled attitude ruin Kasey's excitement at finding a New York Pizzeria that served Hawaiian, handed him a slice. "Ricky, you really have to experience more of life's little adventures."

He stomped his foot in anger. "I hate being called Ricky. Mother named me Horace and that is what I demand to be called."

Val laughed. She found pleasure in teasing him, considering it the best way to break through the wall of resentment that he wore like a sackcloth of misery around his size 14 ½ neck.

"Ah, but your father named you Ricardo, after your Italian grandfather, and Ricky is my Americanized version of that middle name."

"But, it lacks dignity."

Val insisted. "C'mon, the Hawaiian won't kill you. Remember the house rule, two bites of everything."

Horace reluctantly put the pizza on his plate and wiped his fingers on the cloth napkin that neatly covered his lap. Picking up his knife and fork he meticulously cut a slice, and in continental style, took a bite. He chewed carefully and expressed a slight aversion at the taste. Val reminded him, "One bite down, one to go." All eyes were riveted on him so he tried another nibble and realized he enjoyed the sweetness of the pineapple mixed with the chewiness of the ham and the tartness of the sauce. He gulped down the entire slice and held out his plate for more.

Noticing that everyone was smiling at him he cheered up, which often happened in this vibrant household. Georgia's motto of "loving, caring and sharing" remained incomprehensible to him. His middle class New Jersey upbringing by a despondent sixty-three-year-old mother and an impervious seventy-five year-old father, left him outwardly impassive, but inside he ached. His parents always blamed their troubles on someone other than themselves. No one in his neighborhood of heavy drinkers encouraged their children to seek education beyond high school. Considering the adversity in which Horace was raised, he was accomplished. He put himself through two years of college, and moved to New York. He felt fortunate to have found Georgia's ad for an inexpensive apartment that included a part-time job as a cook and handyman. He was astounded by her painfully honest appraisal of him at his third interview when she laid down her expectations.

"I am accepting you on the condition that you attend all my monthly "Gatherings" and are actively involved in the discussions." Horace had no problem with attending a few parties. He might meet some interesting people. He nodded and prepared to exit before she changed her mind but she continued, "And you are to enroll at Baruch in their BBA program."

Head raised in superiority he responded haughtily, "I do not require a degree in business. I am a writer. I have a position on Wall Street researching and editing for a financial bank. I am doing exceptionally well."

10

She disagreed with bluntness, "No Horace, you aren't. You've improved yourself but you have a long way to go to achieve the potential that I see in you." She gave him what he eventually called 'the look'. Her right eyebrow rose, she cocked her head, and with a knowing smile that took the sting out of her words, said, "You come from a substandard background, and you know it. Education that allows you to compete in the harsh reality of the business world is necessary if you want to earn a living that will allow you to spend free time writing."

He felt like arguing that he was more successful than anyone in his family, but he held his tongue as she went on. "I've chosen Baruch because you can self-design your program. Your job on Wall Street allows you to obtain one credit for every six months of work, which means you can graduate with a Bachelor in Business Administration in three years."

He looked at her and pondered the pros and cons. She waited. "Those are my terms. Do you agree?" She had him hooked. He nodded. Her blue eyes sparkled, and she grinned. The next day he moved in and wished he had found her sooner.

After finishing the entire pizza Horace turned to Kasey and asked, "What is your objective for tomorrow? The weather is predicted to be 82 degrees and sunny."

"I'm going job hunting, and if there's time, I want to find a community college with classes that don't start until mid July so I'll have enough money to enroll. Do you have any suggestions as to where I should look?"

Horace, keen to show off his knowledge, answered, "There is the Borough of Manhattan Community College near my work. I can obtain a summer catalogue and inquire about admission on a full-time basis in the fall. That will leave you free to pursue your job search. Where are you going to look, at an office?"

"No, I'm a people person, I'm going to look for work in a deli."

He was aghast. "Why that is beneath you! In New York delis are run by minorities, not people of your caliber."

"How dare you! I'll have you know that I grew up working in my parents' delicatessen. I respect individuals with a work ethic, and that includes people who pick up garbage and sweep the streets. I value people for who they are no matter what their job."

Val applauded her spunk. "Chocolate cream pie anyone? It's just desserts don't you think?" Horace missed the jibe because he was thinking about his younger brother, Christian, who sponged off his mother and him whenever he left a job, which was often. Kasey would be a welcome addition to Georgia's unusual group of family and friends.

He had grown to love, he supposed that was the word, Georgia, John and Val. He also enjoyed many of Georgia's students, alumni, friends and neighbors who came and went at will. He wondered if all theatre professors were like enormous magnets that drew people to them or if it was just Georgia's giving personality. When the doorbell rang, he wasn't quite sure what he would find. Would it be someone crying on the doorstep needing help? Or someone dancing on the stoop because they had been cast in a Broadway show. It was both disconcerting and exciting.

After the dishes were dried and put away they went to their respective rooms to prepare for Monday. Val gathered her semiprofessional 1998 Canon XL1 camcorder and home-sewn tool belt loaded with multiple lenses. Various other accouterments she placed in her bright red backpack that stood out like a stop sign and often saved her from getting hit by a delivery boy on a speeding bicycle.

Georgia spent the evening cleaning her eight-year-old nephew's room. She hadn't seen Nick since last summer and wondered how much he had grown. She made a list of games and library books to get until she had time to take him shopping.

Kasey, with Horace's help, marked up a walking map of the various neighborhoods between school and home. She was determined to find a job and Horace was delighted that he could be of importance to someone.

Horace had almost given up hope that things were ever going to get better for him and rubbed his head in annoyance whenever Georgia insisted that therapy and advanced education would help him "Open a New Window." He hated it when she quoted musical theatre titles in her daily advising sessions because it demonstrated his lack of knowledge in a subject he knew little about. He also scorned her belief that he needed therapy, but he did have to admit she had been right about the business school at Baruch.

In the beginning, Horace felt inferior working on Wall Street. His entry-level job as a research assistant didn't require artistic writing or poetry, two areas he was convinced he excelled in. He got off to a bad start with his co-workers when he bragged about his talent in writing free verse poetry, a genre that Robert Frost likened to "playing tennis without a net." His attitude of superiority caused colleagues to avoid him and he ate lunch alone. Georgia's insistence that he enroll in business courses gave him the education necessary to ask intelligent questions of his co-workers. He was finally being included in lunchtime gatherings.

He had to admit that this tenacious professor was changing him as well as her students. She had rules and standards, and her honest response whenever he bemoaned his lot in life could not be argued with. At times, he wasn't sure if she was putting him down or praising him so he tended to give a half-hearted smile when she burst out with one of her favorite sayings, "Has potential needs work." She urged him, on a weekly basis, to see a therapist. As he sat in his room he tried to think of some way out of her constant harping on therapy. His eyes fell on the Baruch summer catalogue and he thought that they must have summer classes in psychology. He thumbed through the index and was elated to find a second term summer course in Family Psychology.

This would surely get her off his back. What a timely break, two birds with one stone. Pleased with himself, he turned to the course description and noted it was one of the classes of highlighted suggestions she had recommended three years ago. He began to rub his head in irritation but stopped, rolled his eyes to the ceiling, sighed and knew he was fortunate that she cared.

Chapter 3

New York, New York

Kasey walked down Ninth Avenue through the Village, stopping at every deli along the way, and the answer was always the same, "nope." After eight hours of "nope," she was ready to give up when she spied Colleen's Sandwich Shop. She crossed the street and entered a homey eatery boasting green and white-checkered curtains with matching tablecloths. A plump middle-aged woman leaned behind the counter. "Saints preserve us, ya' must be Irish with that red hair and those freckles. Where ya' from, and what's ya' name? Have a seat. M' dogs are barkin'."

Kasey was relieved when the woman handed her a soda and sat with her at one of the seven immaculately clean tables.

"I'm Kasey and you're right about the Irish. My folks owned a Deli in Wilmington, Delaware where I worked from the time I was eight-years-old."

"I'm Colleen Murphy, and darlin', you're a blessing." She made a quick sign of the cross. "When can you start? M' daughter up and gave me a grandson three weeks ago and moved to New Jersey. I been holdin' things together by a shoestring and kin use a good worker."

So Kasey and Colleen figured out a schedule that initially gave Kasey forty hours a week that could be adjusted when her classes began. Both women were ecstatic and after she spent the remaining hour learning the routine, Kasey headed home, exhausted but exhilarated.

She found Horace, Val and Georgia in the bright red kitchen that boasted vibrant yellow cupboards, multicolored counters, and stainless steel commercial appliances. It was an anniversary present from John, who before leaving on one of his consulting trips gave Georgia his credit card and said, "Have fun." He returned three weeks later to find the effervescent new room and Horace, her latest humanitarian project. Georgia, Val and Horace often worked together experimenting with different recipes. Tonight was Chicken Saltimbocca, Horace's favorite.

Kasey told them the news. "I got a job that starts tomorrow and best of all it's near school." The timer rang and everyone brought the food to the table. Horace was in an unusually happy mood, surrounded by three intriguing women and ready to partake of his favorite food. He insisted on playing maitre d' and holding out everyone's chair. Georgia said, "Why don't you sit at the head of the table tonight? John and Nick will be home tomorrow so it's your last chance to play "Master of the House." Val smiled for she recognized the song title from *Les Miz* a musical that starred one of Georgia's dearest friends.

Val was anxious for Kasey to hear about John. "You'll love my dad. He grew up on a dairy farm in New Hampshire where life was harsh. When he was eleven, his father told him there would be no Christmas present that year. They couldn't afford it. Dad spent Christmas crying in the cow barn. That was the day he vowed that his children would have a better life. He started working at nearby resort hotels until he saved enough money to attend the state university where Mom worked."

Georgia continued the story. "John fell in love with me the first time he saw me backstage in a theatre. He was a twenty-three-year-old senior engineering major, and I was a twenty-eight-year-old theatre teacher yelling at forty people to 'buffalo stage left!'. He wanted to take me to the prop loft and bed me right there because strong women did not intimidate him."

Horace, embarrassed by the bedding comment and confused by the "buffalo" dance term, played with his food.

"As we knew each other better he envied my quick wit, honest answers and my determination. We also had the same ethics and love of all types of people, no matter how rich or poor. One thing to remember when choosing a partner is to pick someone with a similar background so you're able to communicate. Speaking the same language helps too, not simply verbal, but a compatible value system." She left to get the dessert, pineapple upside down cake, a '50s favorite of her father's.

Horace was intrigued by the honest relationship Georgia had with John, her husband of nearly thirty years. He wanted to be like John. He had also grown up poor but where John was receptive to people Horace wasn't. He didn't know why. He yearned for a change in his life. After one failed marriage and a few short and disappointing relationships with women, Georgia had urged therapy, which he rejected, telling her he had tried it once and the therapist ended up sleeping with him. Georgia ridiculed his statement telling him the woman was unethical or he was lying. He was most upset when she eyed him and asked, "Or was it a man?"

Georgia was known as a giver of tough love. Her honest responses to her students were often daunting, but they learned to accept criticism because they knew she cared and loved them despite their differences. Georgia was very much like her father who had a similar sense of humor and love of humanity. Her brother, Robert, reminded her of Horace. Both men were insecure about themselves and their masculinity. Thus they were easy prey for deceitful women.

After her father's death, Georgia became her eighty-seven-year-old mother's primary caregiver with power of medical attorney. Despite her quiet mother's aversion to the chaos of Georgia's household, the two became very close. When Roberta lay dying for a week in the hospital, she often asked when Robert was coming but he never did. He never explained why and Georgia was irate at him for hurting their tiny, highly intelligent and well-read 5'1" silver-haired mother who loved him most. She hadn't spoken to her brother since. It was John's idea to have her nephew visit them in New York.

Beginning in 1998, John made Nick's annual summer travel arrangements. In order to prevent seeing Robert's wife, John met Robert and Nick at the airport rather than at their San Francisco home. John had a strong aversion to Arrawika, who was an exploitive, complaining, conniving liar, all traits John detested. He felt the summers Nick spent with them were helping the boy become straightforward, decent and truthful, so he would accompany him on the flight from San Francisco to Newark. The two had bonded and enjoyed each other's company, for Uncle John took a sincere interest in him, something his father did not.

Georgia returned with dessert and they all dug in. The women talked about Val's dream of being a photojournalist but Horace's mind was elsewhere. Georgia interrupted his daydreaming. "See you in the morning. The last one up turns out the lights."

Kasey was concerned that Nick might be in his teens and asked, "How old is this nephew?"

"He's been coming here since he was five and this is my third year, so he must be eight."

A relieved Kasey ran blithely up the stairs. "Looks like you're the last one up." Horace smiled as he watched her go to her room. He shut off the lights and gamboled to his fourth floor apartment.

Chapter 4

Home Again

At 6:00 P.M. on Thursday night Kasey heard urgent banging on the front door. She peeked out the window to see a cab driver setting two suitcases on the sidewalk in front of the house. Paying him was a bespectacled middle-aged, grey-haired man that looked like Bill Gates. The banging on the door continued.

Kasey yelled to Horace, who was busy making spaghetti sauce. "Horace, there's a young, skinny boy banging on the front door. Is that Nick?"

Horace ran to open the door as Nick gave him the high five greeting. John followed, lugging two large suitcases. Nick folded his arms and looked at Kasey. "Who are you?"

Kasey returned the rude greeting by folding her arms and taking the same tone of voice. "I'm Kasey, who are you?"

He got the message and grinned back showing two newly grown front teeth. Nick was a handsome child, a perfect mix of Asian and American. Kasey turned to John with a twinkle in her eye. "And what brings Bill Gates our way?"

John laughed. "Sorry to say, I am no Bill Gates; but you're not the first one to make that mistake. When I fly on certain airlines the flight attendants think I'm travelling under an assumed name, flirt with me unmercifully and upgrade me to first class. It's very helpful. In reality, I'm John, Georgia's husband. You must be Kasey; she told me you had moved in, or rather she had moved you in."

"I hope you don't mind."

"Mind! If I minded the things Georgia did she'd have left me years ago. Where is she by the way?"

Horace checked his watch. "On her way home from a rehearsal. She's trying to convince her students they are ready to perform an improvisational forty-five minute play based on difficult personal experiences. She said to eat without her." John looked down at Nick and said, "I hope you've improved in the eating department since you came last year." Nick looked abashed. John reminded him "Remember, two bites of everything." Nick rolled his eyes and indicated agreement while John and Horace shared a knowing look that implied, "here we go again."

Horace took the suitcases and led the boy upstairs. "C'mon Nick. Georgia's painted your room bright orange and you'll be sharing a bathroom with Kasey. But if you want, you can always come up and use mine." The two started up the stairs chatting like two old friends.

Georgia arrived home after everyone but John had gone to bed. She greeted him with a passionate kiss as he handed her a Sea Breeze, her favorite summer drink. He raised his gin and tonic, "Together again."

She sank on the couch next to him, "I missed you. Three weeks is too long to be celibate and apart. I hate your new consulting job."

He replied, "I know, but it will help me retire at the same time you do at a much more lucrative pension. Think of adventure traveling while we're still vigorous enough to enjoy it. The Trans Siberian Railway?"

"I'll have to study conversational Russian. I might not be up to that language."

He thought of his dream trip. "We'll safari in Africa."

She laughed. "Photography, not guns, I trust."

He knew she hated it when he went deer hunting in New Hampshire. Her worse-case-scenario-mind insisted on believing a drunken hunter would kill him. She anxiously awaited his annual call and breathed in relief when she heard his cheery voice joking, "Bambi lives another year." She and Val relaxed until the following fall when the routine repeated itself.

Georgia finished her Sea Breeze. "You know, when we retire we should take one of those old Catskill hotels and turn it into a summer theatre. I'll direct and you can handle the scenic elements."

John had been through it before. "It doesn't sound much like retirement to me. Life with you is a constant adventure of exploding firecrackers. But what else could I expect being married to a woman born on the fourth of July? Just think, when you get old I can rewrite George M. Cohan's lyric and sing 'you're a grand old hag'...."

Georgia laughed. "You always were off key, but I still love you."

He grinned as she moved to his lap and kissed him passionately. "Hmmm, that tasted good, let's go to bed. I've missed you way too much."

She stood up and pulled him into her arms so their bodies touched. "You feel ready," she quipped, "very ready."

He held her away and looked into her eyes, "Not yet, honey. We have something to discuss that's serious, and I need you to think about it because it's a decision that only you can make. You know I'll support you no matter what."

Worried, she sat back down. "What is it?"

"Robert wants a divorce."

She was thrilled, "It's about time he wised up. What's the problem?"

"You have to make a decision about Nick."

"What decision? He's here. We can just pick up where we left off. Hopefully that kid's not back to square one with refusing to eat to get attention."

John shook his head. "It's not that simple. Your brother is afraid his wife will get custody of Nick."

Georgia was aghast. "Is he stupid? Don't answer that. Of course he is. He married her. Sometimes I think men's brains are six inches below their belts. Present company excluded."

He laughed knowing she was off on a tirade but listened patiently, understanding how angry she was.

"How can Robert possibly think she'll get custody when Arrawika's a gambling, lying, cheating, alcoholic? She's an unfit mother in anyone's book. No judge in her right mind would award her custody."

John agreed. "That's what we know. Remember your insecure brother will vacillate and not take any action until it's too late. He reminds me of Horace, oblivious and absolutely clueless about women. Remember the different Thai military men she slept with? They left her with three sons that she said were her younger brothers."

"I don't understand how he could be so stupid. How are we involved? Does he want us to testify on his behalf?"

"No, he wants to know if we will keep Nick until he gets things straightened out. It may take a while."

"Whew! What a life change! Val graduates and Nick arrives. Imagine raising an eight-year-old at age fifty-nine? There goes retirement while we're young enough to enjoy it."

John gazed at her. "What are you considering?"

She smiled a coquettish grin and her blue eyes sparkled like a conniving teenager. "That I won't get much sleep and I've a great idea for escaping thinking. Let's see if making love will take priority over brooding. Bet you anything it does."

John grabbed her hand. "Forget the lights let's just go to bed." They both glowed as they dashed up the stairs like two nineteen-year-olds, deeply in love and very much ready for bed.

Chapter 5

Accentuate the Positive

In early July, Georgia threw her first "Student, Alumni and Friends Gathering" of the summer and reminded Horace that he had to attend and verbally participate, at least once. The conversation centered on last week's Gay Pride Day march. The topic made Horace extremely nervous because his ex-wife had accused him of being less than a man in bed. He worried that some in the group might think he was gay, so he sat on the steps, far removed from the rest.

Georgia started the discussion with one of her famous 'I was there' stories. "The first Gay Pride march in 1970 was created to mark the anniversary of the Stonewall riots. We all assembled on Christopher Street and walked to Central Park. I was twenty-eight and realized it was time to take a human rights stand.

"The parade began as a small nervous gathering that grew in numbers as it proceeded without incident. At exactly 3:00 P.M. everyone froze. There was a full minute of absolute silence to honor all those who had been affected by being gay." Sandy, a first year graduate student asked, "How were they affected back then? AIDS didn't become prevalent until the mid 80's."

Forty-eight-year-old Eleanor responded, "Gays were physically brutalized by macho men and harassed by the police if they entered a mafia owned Village bar that didn't pay the correct amount of 'protection' money. I had several friends hospitalized after ferocious beatings by the enforcers of the law."

Georgia asked, "Teddy, were you at the first Gay Pride Day march? You're about the right age."

"Naturally, I was there; I was seventeen and it was a not-to-be missed event. So while I didn't understand everything that was going on, I remember the moment of silence. It was eerie and very moving. We've come a long way since 1970. As more and more of us admitted we were homosexual we gained more and more civil rights."

Eleanor asked, "Do you ever think the day will come when we see same sex marriage for gay couples."

"A lot more of us are going to have to come out before that happens."

Georgia turned to the subject of coming out. Horace's palms began to sweat which they often did when he got nervous. He wanted an excuse to leave the room but saw Georgia watching him, so he rubbed his head and avoided her look.

"Who wants to tell their coming out story?"

Joel, one of her cutest male students, started the discussion. "Well, I didn't have any problem at all."

Others in the room looked skeptical, both male and female, ranging in age from eighteen to seventy-five.

"Yeah, right."

"Like I believe that."

The twenty-two-year-old laughed. "It's true. It was my freshman year in college. I was from a small town in Vermont and had done some musicals for a community theatre where my mom sewed costumes, folded programs, swept the stage, just about anything that was needed."

Sandy said, "Stick to the story!"

"Sorry. Well, she and dad drove me to school, moved me into my dorm and headed back home. An hour later the phone rang. It was mom telling me they had arrived safely and then she paused." The suspense built. " 'Joel, I have a question to ask you.' 'Sure Mom, what is it?' 'Joel, are you gay?' I thought should I lie to her? Why is she asking this? Something told me I'd feel better if she knew. 'Yes, I am.' Then she said, 'I just wanted to know. Talk to you next week. Good luck, bye.' And that was that."

Others greeted his comment with amazement. Horace knew his parents would have hurled him from the house after a severe beating from his father and a lot of cursing and crying from his mother. Randy, the cruise line choreographer was envious. "You were luckier than most of us in the room. I'm forty-eight and still haven't told my dad. I didn't even know I was gay until I was twenty and a sophomore in college. I had lots of friends who were girls and their parents loved having me around." Everyone laughed. "I went to all the proms and kissed all my dates goodnight. Everything I was supposed to do, but I had no desire to take things further. In fact, it wasn't until summer stock that I first thought I should bed this girl who was after me hot and heavy."

Georgia reminded them, "I always advise against summer stock romances. The pace is too intense."

"I wish you told me that. Maybe you did but I didn't hear it. I *am* a Tenor you know."

Eleanor joked, "And a blonde to boot."

"At any rate, this girl went after me in a big way, and I was ready to go all the way. At the last minute she said, 'Did you bring any protection?' When I said 'no,' she got up and threw me out of her room. A few days later one of the tech guys drove me home and after a few beers and some fast advances on his part, I realized I was a homosexual. The girl cornered me three days later and waved a condom in my face. She said she was ready. I informed her that I was gay. She looked at me in disbelief and blamed herself, thinking I would have been straight if she had gone to bed with me that first night. She spent the rest of the summer trying to chase me down. It was crazy."

Horace found himself wondering why no girl had ever gone after him in a big way. Well, not until Emma found him on the Internet. He felt his tension subside at the thought that a woman on the other side of the world yearned for him.

Kasey asked Georgia, "Why do people deceive themselves of true happiness because of the opinions of others especially their families?

Horace knew that his mother's opinion mattered more than anyone else's and he worried that she would think he was gay if he didn't marry someone very soon. He had received many tongue-lashings from her over the years but the subject of homosexuality had not yet been raised and he wanted to make sure it never did.

Georgia said, "We put too much emphasis on the traditional family." Val, who had been videoing the entire evening, turned off her camera and suggested, "Why don't we create a new definition for the word family?"

There was silence as everyone considered the idea.

Junie, a fun loving, spirited girl said, "I'm for it. I was thrown out of the house at age fourteen because my parents discovered I had lost my virginity and they didn't want me contaminating my sisters."

Margaret said, "You aren't the only one who didn't fit into the acceptable mold. I rebelled against going to Mass and listening to the known pedophiliac priest rant on about hell and damnation, something my parents reinforced with Sunday beatings. I left for New York and never turned back."

Allen, age twenty-five, added, "Try being gay in the Bible Belt and see how your family overreacts. Hey, why don't we all write down one sentence of what each of us feels is important in a family?

Joel came up with a name. "We can call it the 'eclectic family'. Eclectic means diverse and when I look around this room I see a diverse group."

Val added, "That title works for me because eclectic also means free."

Teddy agreed, "We can lay out all our sentences, put them in some kind of order and see what we come up with.

The group created the following viable interpretation they all agreed on:

The 'eclectic family' is created by choice of the participants rather than DNA. These are people of assorted ages that make an impact on who you are or will be. They enjoy being together and comprise the 'relatives' you choose, based on demonstrated trust and love. This diverse family is one you cherish because they are honest with you when you are at your worst, which will help you become your best.

Horace wondered if he would ever have enough friends for an eclectic family. The idea was appealing, because he didn't like or respect most of his DNA relations but he worried about what his mother would say. Georgia, tired of waiting for him to verbally participate, moved to his side. He knew he better say something before she humiliated him. He cleared his throat and said, "Here, here!" Georgia gave him 'the look' and he turned his head away from her disparaging eyes.

It was late, and everyone began to leave in pairs or small groups, continuing the discussion as they walked onto 22nd Street where the roses from the garden were sweet and the night was perfect for walking and talking. This was July of 2001, and a certain feeling of safety gave confidence to area residents. It was a great time to be alive, and nobody could ask for a more vibrant city than New York.

Chapter 6

Fireworks

It was July 4th. Kasey and Horace were busy preparing Georgia's birthday dinner when the phone rang. Horace answered. It was the 99-cent store on 23rd Street calling for Georgia. As she was upstairs Horace raised his voice and yelled, "Georgia!"

She stuck her towel wrapped body out the bathroom door, "Yes?"

He looked away murmuring, "Sorry."

She laughed at his embarrassment. "Honestly Horace haven't you ever seen your mother wrapped in a towel? Jeeez Louise." Without waiting for him to reply, for his face answered for him, she asked, "What's up?"

He replied quickly, for he had never seen his mother scantily dressed, "It's the manager of the 99-cent store calling for you. Something about Nicholas."

Georgia grabbed the phone from his outstretched hand. Her face grew angry. "I'll be there in five minutes,"

Horace watched her run back upstairs. In less than three minutes she ran out the door dressed in blue jeans and a red and white striped shirt. The door slammed behind her.

She arrived at the 99-cent store to find Nicholas looking as if he was superior to the Spanish-speaking manager.

Georgia grabbed Nick's arm. "What did you take?"

Nick smiled in an attempt to appeal to her good nature. "It was nothing,"

Her anger built as she repeated, "What did you take?"

He replied in a casual manner, "Only some decorations for your birthday party. All the kids steal. In California and here too."

Realizing he saw no wrong in what he did she ordered the manager, "Call the cops. We are not thieves. There are no robbers allowed in our house. We work for our money and if we cannot afford something we do not take it." She glared at Nick who looked uncomfortable but showed no remorse. She repeated in crystal clear diction that she used when angry. "Call the cops."

The manager reminded her, "But, Messes. Hogan, thees ees Quarto de Julio."

"I don't care if it's Easter Sunday, Christmas Day or Buddha's birthday. Call the cops and tell them there is a robbery going on."

The manager pressed a button and within minutes a patrol car with flashing lights screeched to a stop in front of the store. A burly cop got out, and Nick finally looked scared. Georgia met him at the door.

"Officer, this is my nephew, who is stealing from this store. I want you to talk to him and see if he should be arrested."

"Should I use the cuffs?"

Georgia eyed Nick, who was now shaking in fear. "It doesn't matter to me, but you look big enough to handle him without them. If he tries to run, you can always shoot him." Nick's eyes bulged at the words 'shoot him'. The officer took the petrified young man to the patrol car. "I'll see if he has any other offenses."

"He's from California so check the San Francisco area."

Five minutes later, Nicholas, in tears, reappeared with the policeman. "No record anywhere else. Usually we let people go on a first offense. The jails are full this time of year. So I'll leave him in your custody. And I don't want to see you again, young man."

Nicholas stammered, "N…N…N…No officer."

Georgia turned to the manager. "How much does he owe you."

"Ten dolares."

Georgia handed him fifty dollars, "For what he stole, the phone call and your trouble. Thank you for calling me." She glared at Nick, reminding him, "We do not steal, ever."

She pulled him from the store without saying a word and dragged him into the Korean market. Georgia walked up to the storeowner, "Lee, this is my nephew who is staying with us for the summer. He stole from the store up the street, and I am ashamed to say he is a thief. You are not to let him in your store unless he is with me or another adult from our home."

Georgia looked at Nick who was very quiet. She felt he had learned his lesson, but just to make sure she took him to the video store and repeated the same tirade to Benny, the owner. Then she pulled him home and into the door of their 22nd street home where Kasey and Horace were waiting.

She ordered him upstairs. "Go to your room and think about what you have done. Be glad Val isn't here to film your shame and our family's dishonor. I'll be up later to talk to you. Remember in the Shultze-Hogan house we do not condone thievery, and we do not have liars or thieves among us."

Kasey asked, "What happened?" Georgia filled them in.

Horace was horrified at her treatment of the youngster. "How could you humiliate him like that?"

She shot him 'the look'. "How could I not? It's a lesson he should have learned years ago from his parents. But that's asking a lot of his deceitful mother, who probably stole much more than party decorations from the men she rolled in upstairs bar bedrooms."

Her anger escalated. "My idiot brother, who acts like an ostrich with his head stuck in a book instead of the sand, married her for better or worse and the situation is much worse. She sees him as a walking ATM machine." Georgia looked at her watch; her venting was over. "I better talk to him. He's been alone long enough."

She went upstairs as John came through the door carrying a large, poorly wrapped present tied in a red, white and blue bow. "What's been happening while I've been at the office?"

Horace, sure that John would find her behavior appalling, answered, "Nick got in trouble stealing from the 99-cent store, and do you know what she did to him?"

"I know just what she did. Called the cops, grabbed Nick, took him around to the neighborhood stores and introduced him as a thief she was embarrassed to know."

"How did you guess?"

Val overheard the exchange and added, "Because that's what she did to me when I was fourteen and did the same thieving thing."

Horace was aghast at Val's complacency,

"Didn't you hate her for that?"

Val shook her head. "No, it was the best thing she ever did. I learned not to want things I couldn't afford. If I desired something I had to get a job. I think that little incident gave me the work ethic I have today. It certainly gave me a strong value system."

Georgia returned with Nick, who ran to give the man he respected more than any other a big hug, "I'm sorry Uncle John."

John ruffled the boy's hair in forgiveness. "I know it won't happen again so let's start the celebration by watching *Yankee Doodle Dandy* and I promise not to sing along with Jimmy Cagney." Everyone relaxed as Horace passed out cups of popcorn and cans of soda. Georgia and John crowded on the sofa with Nick squeezed in between. The others lay on the floor to enjoy the black and white video for Georgia, like Jimmy Stewart, hated the "colorized" versions of old movies.

Later, they watched the fireworks on TV. At 10:00 P.M., they sat around the dinner table eating cake and ice cream. John said, "I guess this is the time you tell your stories of growing up in the '50's."

Val set up her camera.

Nick loved the tradition, "Dad never tells us any childhood stories because he would rather read to himself than spend time with me."

Val reminded her, "Keep it natural Mom; it's film not one of your drama classes."

Georgia began quietly, "Robert and I were among the "perfect" '50's elder brother/younger sister family. My parents, although they loved us both, had their favorites. Robby, the easier and geekier of us, gravitated to my quiet, former Latin teacher, Mom, while I, the fun loving, pushing the envelope younger, was Dad's constant companion. Mom would often look at me and say, 'If you had been born first we never would have had your brother,' or 'if you didn't look so much like your father's side of the family I would think there was a mix-up in the hospital.'

"Today child psychologists would have Mom arrested for emotional child abuse but I understood my very staid, proper mother was confused by my uniqueness. Actually it was ADHD, but no one knew what that was back then.

"Our high school was small so we often had the same teachers, some of whom would point out my lack of concentration. One was particularly exasperating and kept asking, 'Why can't you be more like your brother? He's so studious.' I shut her up in no uncertain terms with the statement, Robert may be more studious but I have a better personality, now *whom* do you think will go further in life? I was never compared to him again." Everyone laughed.

"Robert became a person of note in his final year of high school when I became his campaign manager, and he was elected president of the student body. The thing that confused me was how much torture this person of note went through when asking a girl to a prom. I used to listen at the door when he and his best friend Davey would run down the alphabetical list of the girls in his class. The conversation would go something like this…."

And she proceeded to give a dramatic rendition using two separate male voices.

ROBERT: "What about Jane Maddow?"

DAVEY: "Nah, she's a dog."

ROBERT: "The next one is Nancy Nadeau."

DAVEY: "She's goin' steady with the football captain."

ROBERT: "Well, we can forget Linda Oliver, she's got Joe's ring."

DAVEY: "How about Polly Plumber?"

ROBERT: "No, I heard she got thrown out of school because she's pregnant."

DAVEY: "No kiddin! Wonder who the guy was?"

ROBERT: "It could have been a relative. Her people all work at the mushroom factory and have an outside pump for water."

Kasey's ears perked up at the mention of a mushroom factory and she felt a shiver of fear course through her body. "Excuse me, but where did you grow up?"

"In Wilmington, Delaware." She noticed Kasey stiffen. "Why?"

"The mushroom comment. Please continue."

"Where was I? Well, no matter. Your father reached the letter V; there were only two girls left." She returned to the imitation.

DAVEY: "Whadda' ya think of Naomi Vellors?"

ROBERT: "She's OK, but I took her last year. Why don't you take her this year? That way she won't get any ideas that I'm interested."

DAVEY: "All right. Susan Weston is last so you'll have to take her unless you want to me to start all over."

ROBERT: "No, She's OK Do you think she'll say yes?"

DAVEY: "Yeah."

Val noticed Horace yawning. "Bedtime for Rick and Nick. And if Kasey works tomorrow, I'll read Nick a book and clean up."

Everyone started up the stairs to their rooms as Georgia took John's hand, "Come on, I'll open that sexy negligee in private."

Val filmed her them as they turned and blew her a kiss goodnight. She stored the tapes marked 'Mom's sixtieth birthday' in a fireproof safe in the hall closet. In a few hours, the house was quiet except for the sound of neighborhood sporadic fireworks.

Georgia snuggled closer to a sleeping John and lay awake thinking. She had a lot on her mind and deliberated about Nick. As a firecracker popped in the distance, she realized that the only chance the poor kid had for parental attention and love was if he stayed in New York. Today's transgression proved that he needed to be in a firm but loving environment. She looked with fondness at her snoring husband and knew they could raise Nick as well as they had raised Val. She thought back on their life together and realized that despite the difference in their ages (she was older by five years) they had much in common especially the gift of accepting people's foibles.

Unable to sleep she walked to the window seat and watched the occasional firework flare and thought back to Christmas of 1993 when Nick was one-year-old and Robert's family was visiting their parents' home in Orlando.

She could still see Val and Grandpa Rudy sitting next to each other on the living room couch, Grandpa in his red sweater and Val in her red dress reading aloud from *Horton Hatches the Egg*. Grandpa Rudy, who idolized his only granddaughter, laughed and applauded as she took on the various character voices. Maisie was his favorite. The turkey and dressing roasted in the oven.

Arrawika, anxious for attention, disgusted everyone when she removed Robert's shoes and socks and began clipping his toenails over grandpa's unread newspaper. The timer rang as Grandma Roberta announced, "Time to wash up, the turkey's almost ready and dinner will be on the table in twenty minutes."

Robert looked up from his book, and in his maddeningly slow, speaking voice, asked, "Where is there a Chicken take-out?"

Grandpa Rudy said, "Why?"

Robert peered at him through his thick, horn-rimmed glasses. "Arrawika doesn't eat turkey."

Grandpa Rudy, who had been in the food business all his life, responded with irritation. "What the hell's the difference? Sorry, Val. If we weren't going to eat so soon I'd take a nap."

Georgia chuckled at the memory, because that was her beloved dad's way of coping. He slept a lot the week Robert and Arrawika visited. She thought a few seconds more, and as a firecracker popped in the distance, she remembered looking at Nick in his playpen and wondering, "What will his future be like with those two as his parents?"

At that moment she knew what her decision would be. She shook the memory from her mind, crawled into bed and threw an arm around her sleeping husband, who opened his eyes, turned and murmured, "Hmm?"

"I've decided that Nick is staying with us. Go back to sleep you loving man."

Chapter 7

Adventure

Georgia and John were members of various museums around the city; many had weeklong, summer programs for children. Shortly after Georgia's birthday Nick entered his room to find various "adventure week" colorful brochures strewn across his bed. He spent two hours researching and moving different ones to a pile of favorites. He could learn to paint, sculpt, weave, study the solar system, participate in the production of a play or experience various foreign languages. The offerings were numerous and each one was written to entice both children and adults.

Georgia came into the room just as he finished the last brochure. There were many words he didn't understand but he handed her the pictorial descriptions that interested him the most. She sat next to him and asked, "Well, what do you think?"

Nick handed her four from the Museum of Natural History, his favorite museum in New York. She read, "Hands-on Learning: Human Evolution Through the Study of Fossils and DNA. Do you understand the term 'DNA'?"

He replied, "Sure Mom watches TV all day long and sometimes I watch with her. I like *Law and Order* and they have a new spinoff called *Law and Order: SVU*."

Georgia felt her blood begin to boil, "Special Victims Unit is on at 9:00 P.M. on a school night. Why aren't you in bed? Where's your father? Who helps you with your homework?"

Her questions spewed forth as quickly as bullets from a Gatling gun and Nick felt she was blaming him. He began to cry.

"I'm sorry, Nick; I didn't mean to upset you." She moved from the window seat to the bed where she sat next to her sniffling nephew and handed him a tissue. "I'm really not angry with you at all."

He hung his head and hunched his shoulders. "Why not? I'm the one who stays up late. I'm the one who goes to school without my homework. It's my fault. It's my most grievous fault. The priest says the age of reason is seven, and I'm eight. I'll be nine on December 24th."

Georgia knew he received no parental attention or guidance and blamed himself for every transgression. She thought if he didn't feel better about himself soon, he would be as self-deprecating as Horace. She decided to spend more time with him. Noticing he was more interested in the brochures and less upset with himself, she chose another one and continued reading aloud, "Spiders Alive: Get Personal and Close to a Tarantula. You like that one?"

He nodded in excitement.

She shuddered as she remembered that Val was petrified of spiders. She thought of a way to get the idea out of his head. "It doesn't say if you bring the Tarantula home to study it 24/7, and I'm going to tell you a secret." She looked around the room, crawled on her knees to check under the bed, opened the closet door, peeked in and shut it. She returned to sit next to him. He waited in wide-eyed anticipation.

"Now don't tell anyone, but Val is petrified of spiders. Ever since she was a little girl, just about your age."

Looking wistful (but loving Val) he shoved the brochure to the bottom of the pile, which left the last two. He wondered which one his aunt would agree to.

She read, pronouncing the words very carefully, "Astrophysics and Bioluminescence are the remaining two. Do you know what they are?"

"Bio something or other is about things that glow in the dark. I've seen fireflies back home, but I've never seen glow-in-the-dark sharks, snails, mushrooms or fish. That sounds neat. In Astro*psychics* I make a rocket. But I don't know why a psychic has anything to do with rockets. I thought they used crystal balls."

"What do you know about psychics?"

Nick answered, "Mom sees one on a weekly basis and takes me along." Seeing the disgusted look on his Aunt's face he sped up. "But I sit outside in the waiting room while they talk for an hour."

Georgia changed the subject back to the workshops. "Let's see." She pretended to be debating and held one brochure in each hand and looked from left to right. "Tell you what, you can take both if you can pronounce the titles correctly."

45

He listened carefully; two meant he didn't need to make a decision. Choices were hard for him because he was afraid of making a mistake. He repeated after her, "Astrophysics and Bioluminescence. Astrophysics and Bioluminescence." This went on for ten repeats, and then she insisted he say the words alone. He messed up and was convinced she wouldn't let him attend either one. He didn't dare look at her for he had failed.

She said with warmth, "It will be easier if we break the words into syllables and turn them into a cheer, the way fans do at sporting events."

He had never been to a sporting event or even seen one on TV, for his mother only watched soap operas and crime dramas. Georgia started clapping her hands and the two created a rhythm - Astro-physics, Bio-lu-mi-ness (they hissed) ence. He followed her lead and they chanted, clapped and foot stamped all the way down the stairs.

John entered with Horace as Nick announced, "I'm taking two camps this summer, in Astro-physics and Bio-lu-mi-nessss-ence." He ended with a skinny-legged leap and they laughed. John smiled at Georgia, knowing she was raising the boy's self-esteem. As Nick handed Horace the brochures, John gave Georgia a kiss and whispered, "You're lucky he picked those two classes since those were the ones you signed him up for last April."

She poked him in the ribs and murmured back, "You know they fill up rapidly. He wanted to take the Tarantula one, but loves Val enough that I was able to get that idea out of his head. It was very close though."

"You won't have to worry about that next year. Nick can pick out his own classes the minute they open up. It will be simpler having him live with us."

Chapter 8

You're Never Fully Dressed Without a Smile

Horace's office was near Kasey's college so he often walked her home. They liked strolling up Fifth Avenue to Bryant Park where they saw old movies or stopped at the midtown library for a lecture. She enjoyed his companionship but neither talked very much. He respected her privacy and she his. One night, Horace commented as they passed the Empire State Building, "I am amazed that you and Georgia talk with such love about your fathers. Val told me that Georgia's personality was very much like Grandpa Rudy's. But all the girls that I have dated are more like their mothers, greedy and exploitive. And my 'ex' was exactly the same way."

Kasey felt like telling him he was dense for seeking out the same type of partner. She looked at him with pity for his pattern of behavior did not differ from that of an abused woman. She wondered about his relationship with his mother, but rather than ask him questions that would make him uncomfortable she said, "I guess you date or marry the wrong women. A girl gains her self-respect from her father and a solid father-daughter relationship is more important for a girl's self esteem than the relationship she has with her mother."

He continued with hesitation, for he rarely asked private questions of others but curiosity got the better of him, "I take it your parents are both deceased?"

His question threw her off balance, and she looked away, pained that she might never see her mother again. She responded, barely above a whisper, "Both are gone. Dad after a lengthy bout of colon cancer and Mom faded away after that."

Horace didn't know how to respond, so they walked the remaining fifteen minutes with an uncomfortable silence between them. When they returned home Horace slipped off his shoes and went to change into something more casual to prepare dinner. Val had her camera on a tripod prepared to film him rushing down the stairs. She knew he hated being late and when he was flustered he dashed to and fro to make up for lost time. When he hurried, he resembled an ostrich, running like a football player with the goal in mind. Val heard him thundering down the three flights of stairs and yelled, "Lights, camera, action!" She turned on the camcorder and was overcome with laughter.

He stopped in a huff. "What do you find so amusing?"

She turned off the camera and sank to the steps as tears streamed down her face. "Ricky, What are you wearing? You look like a mafia drag queen."

Insulted, he responded, "What's wrong with this? It's black, and I look good in black."

Val contained herself and said with determination, "I am taking you shopping right after supper, and it's my treat. You need some serious help in the clothing department. That overly tight shirt with rickrack trim looks like a woman's thrift shop bargain. Does it button on the right or the left?" Horace felt the opening and realized to his horror that he was wearing a woman's shirt. He turned and hurried back to his room as Val shouted with glee, "Be glad I turned off the camera, you don't want archival footage of that do you?"

After dinner, Val dragged Horace to Macy's as Nick, Kasey, John and Georgia agreed to meet them at the Empire State Building. They carried Val's equipment, so she could focus on helping Horace pick out a suit for his annual evaluation. John pressed a few hundred-dollar bills into Val's palm as she and Horace left for Macy's.

They entered the men's department where a portly salesman greeted them. He wore a tape measure around his neck. "May I help you?"

Horace was embarrassed for he had never shopped with a woman before. Val answered, "I'm looking for a nice grey summer-weight wool suit that won't wrinkle and is on sale."

"What size?" Horace had no idea. The salesman eyed his skinny body. "Probably a 34 regular. Let me measure your waist and inseam." He knelt down with his tape measure and reached for Horace's inseam.

Horace jumped away and muttered, "Not here. There must be somewhere more private."

Val was amused because she had seen men backstage in her mother's theatre wearing nothing but their underwear. The salesman looked at her, shrugged and led Horace into the dressing rooms.

A few minutes later the salesman showed Val two suits, one dark grey and one light grey. "While he's trying them on will you please bring some light blue short sleeve shirts, 14 ½ neck, and a satin tie in the same color?"

Horace returned carrying a light grey suit and said, "This is the one I want."

Val was suspicious, for Horace never made quick decisions. "I'm not paying for anything I haven't approved. Go back and put it on so I can see it." She pointed firmly to the dressing room, and Horace returned in the suit he liked best, which Val instantly nixed. "Too tight for business. Let me see the other one."

Horace was downhearted for his Australian girlfriend always talked about his sexy body. He turned and shlumped to the dressing room in a snit. When he returned, an applauding Val greeted him warmly. He straightened up.

"C'mon, Ricky, give me a smile." He looked in the mirror and smiled back at her pleased reflection. Val handed the salesman the money as she whispered to Horace, "You look very handsome!" He began to daydream that he was as handsome as Gary Cooper." Val encouraged him further. "I know your boss will be impressed by your professional look." He continued to admire himself as he took various GQ model positions. Val checked her watch and broke his self-adoration absorption, "Now hurry up, we've got to meet everyone at the Empire State while it's still daylight. I want to film everyone as the lights come on over Manhattan."

They filmed for two hours, and Val made sure to include lots of footage of Nick with her parents as they showed him the different views of the city.

When they returned home, Georgia and John each took one of Nick's hands, and the three moved upstairs to read him Grandpa Rudy's favorite poem, "Casey at the Bat." Nick insisted on three readings and loved it because he realized that Casey was both a male and female name. As he considered that thought, he confided, "You know, I've never, ever been to a baseball game."

Nick said this as Horace passed by the room and popped in, "Never? You have never been to a ball game? I cannot imagine such a thing!" Everyone knew that he was a baseball fan of immense proportions.

John said, "He's crazy for the Mets."

Horace reached in his pocket to show them the baseball card of Tom Seaver, the winner of the 1967 National League Rookie of the Year Award. His green eyes twinkled at Nick as he decided to treat him to his adroitness at magic. "Look, Nick, there's something behind your ear."

Horace, with a quick movement of his hand, reached behind Nick's ear and brought forth his prize baseball card and handed it to him saying, "Here!"

Nick gasped and looked at Rick in amazement. "Where did that come from?"

Horace laughed, gave the young boy his sincerest and biggest smile, and in an eerie voice said, "Ahaaa, It's magic." For the first time, John and Georgia saw a relaxed theatrical side to Horace, who confided to Nick, "Now you have a baseball card of my favorite player. I always dreamed of being a pitcher, but never got any encouragement from my folks." He looked at the card in Nick's hand, "Guess it wasn't in the cards." There was a slight bitterness in his voice, but it ended quickly as he said, "You hang onto that card; it may be a good luck charm for you. Perhaps there is a Mets game somewhere in your future."

John and Georgia smiled at each other because Horace was not known for his generosity. They left for their room as Horace waved goodnight to the excited but sleepy eight-year-old. He thought, if only Georgia and John were my parents, how different my life would have been.

As he turned off the light he saw that Nick was asleep with the poem in one hand and the baseball card in the other. He envisioned the boy dreaming that he was among the crowd in the stands booing because mighty Casey had struck out. He thought a minute and eventually smiled as he imagined it was Tom Seaver who struck him out. For once, Horace felt very good about himself. He knew he would miss his favorite baseball card and not be able to afford a new one for quite a while but the boy's happiness made up for it. He closed the door and smiled wistfully.

Chapter 9

Take a Job

The next day Horace snuck downstairs wearing his new suit, hoping no one would be there to comment. He felt foolish tiptoeing down the steps in his white stocking feet because he knew he resembled Bugs Bunny in one of Nick's favorite cartoons. As he hit the bottom step the family yelled as a unit, "Break a leg." As Nick gave him a high five, Georgia noticed his short socks and gasped, "What are those on your feet?"

"Sport socks. What's wrong with them?"

Val picked up on her mother's thought, "They're white, and they're too short. Go back to your room and get some appropriate length black or grey socks."

John sensed his discomfort and realized that Horace's wardrobe, finances and knowledge of business etiquette were sorely lacking. He told Nick, "Run upstairs to my middle dresser drawer and pick out a few pairs of socks; we can match them to the suit when they're down here."

Nick dashed up the stairs and returned (via the banister railing) seconds later. John approved the socks, and Horace set off, but looked back to see everyone waving from the front steps. It took some of the impending doom from his gloomy walk.

54

An hour later Horace entered the building and went to his office where he waited for his boss, Mr. Flanders. Annual evaluations always panicked him because he only heard a portion of what was said. Horace was a half-listening, well-read daydreamer. Terrified of being fired because he needed both the salary and the one credit business practicum to graduate, his hands began to perspire.

Mr. Flanders, his myopic, fifty-two-year-old, short, rotund, jovial boss smiled as he entered the office. Horace leapt to his feet, hit his knee on the desk and winced in pain. Mr. Flanders held out his hand. Horace hesitated. His nerves made his hands perspire, but he must shake hands with the boss. He hurriedly wiped his palm on his pant leg, shook Mr. Flanders outstretched hand and smiled weakly. His boss motioned for him to sit, which he did.

Mr. Flanders looked at his notepad and began, "You've made wonderful progress during the last year. Your courses at Baruch have improved your relationships with your fellow workers."

Horace didn't absorb anything but the words relationships with fellow workers. He blinked at his boss and wondered, does Mr. Flanders think I'm gay?

Flanders, getting no verbal response, continued, "You're a good writer because you grasp concepts and if given enough time you sometimes produce excellent work. You're also a good editor of our corporate reviews because you don't impose your ideas on the work of others. So you can edit in the style of the author."

These are strong points, but Horace's pessimistic personality only absorbed the word sometimes. Fear rose within him because he was certain the next sentence would be, you're fired. This caused his overstressed mind to worry; where will I get another job? I won't be able to pay my rent or take classes in the fall or finish college. He sighed and thought, so near and yet so far. It is the story of my miserable life.

Mr. Flanders finished speaking of strengths and continued with concern and warmth to give Horace some areas that needed improvement, "Since a portion of your job entails research, it requires an ability to skim in order to glean the salient points of an article. It's a talent that some people have and others do not. Once you finish your degree, you should look for a job that utilizes your strengths. One that does not require either fast reading or accurate spelling."

All Horace heard were the words, "look for a job." He noticed Mr. Flanders was standing with his hand outstretched. Horace stood quickly, wiped his hand on his pant leg and shook his boss's hand. As Mr. Flanders left the office, Horace was not sure if he needed to empty his desk or not, but Mr. Flanders called out to him, "I'll write this up and make sure you have a copy on your desk Monday. See you then." Horace assumed that he still had a job, but he wouldn't be sure until Monday.

He spent the rest of the day trying to improve his skimming skills but found the effort was too great for his brain to absorb. He pondered, daydreamed and worried for the next seven hours. The weekend was going to be dismal and he would not be one hundred percent sure if he still had a job until he arrived at work on Monday. He felt himself spiraling downward and it wasn't even Sunday.

Chapter 10

It's a Helluva Way to Run a Love Affair

Horace headed home, growing more and more despondent the longer he walked. He hated the fact that evaluations were always on Fridays because it forced him to wait two more days to discover if he had a job and the weekend would be agonizing. He decided to walk to the Village and see if any of his buddies were interested in eating or drinking with him. He was desperate for companionship, but didn't want anyone at home to question him about his day. He couldn't face their disappointed faces when he told them he had been sacked. Then he reviewed the situation and wasn't positive he had been fired. Maybe Georgia was right, maybe he did need therapy or at the very least some focus medication. She felt no shame that she was ADHD and once implied that his impaired social interaction skills may be due to Asperger's Syndrome or ADD. He didn't even research the words, because he couldn't tell his mother he had any kind of problem. He worried about what she would think or, even worse, say.

He arrived at the bar and was greeted by a sea of unfamiliar male faces who appeared to be in their thirties. They looked away and focused on each other. Horace was nearly forty and they made him feel much older. He left the bar mired in depression and continued his lonely walk through the Village and Washington Square. He spent a desperate hour reading the posted flyers, hoping there might be an interesting lecture or outdoor concert, but during summer weekends most people left New York for Fire Island or the country. He stopped at Donitelli's Pizza, ordered a calzone and a mug of beer and sat alone at the counter hoping that someone would notice him but nobody did. He nursed the beer for over an hour and made sure he arrived home after everyone was in bed.

He knew his loneliness would end when Emma came to the states and they married. Her e-mails were incredibly literate and it was hard to believe she was a Thai and English was not her first language.

He quickly booted up his computer and found an e-mail waiting.

> From Emma@aol.com
> Subject: I am in love with you
> Date: August 3, 2001   11:10AM ACS
> To: hrTedesco2@aol.com

I am getting a ticket to Washington DC in late November to stay with my Brazilian sister. I am thrilled to be cuming to you forever. I look at your sexy pictures and know we will make beautiful babies together. As I lie in my bathing suit I think of us together and my body grows warm. I am always wet in my sexy two-piece bikinis. They are easy to get on and off, which is why I like them.

> From: hrTedesco2@aol.com
> Subject: You are so far away
> Date: Friday August 3, 2001   11:20PM EDST
> To: Emma@aol.com

I am happy that you enjoy swimming as much as I do. I want to marry someone just like you. Not a materialistic American woman who only wants a man for his money. Can you come to the states sooner?

> From Emma@aol.com
> Subject: I will try
> Date: Friday, August 3, 2001   11:30AM ACS
> To: hrTedesco2@aol.com

I may be in Virginia in September. Your love is so precious to me. Please send me some of your writing so we can have an intellectual discussion. It will help us know each other on a scholarly basis, which is of utmost importance if we are to marry.

Horace was overwhelmed. Emma's philosophy was the same as Georgia's. He felt proud that he was sharing his deepest thoughts with a girl who had as much wisdom and class as Georgia, someone he held in deepest regard. Maybe Emma would visit in September and see what a wonderful New York family he lived with. He turned off the computer and prepared for bed in a romantic and excited mood.

Chapter 11

The Truth

Kasey and Horace did well in their summer classes, and without homework and term papers, they had weekends free to spend time with Nick and Val, visiting various museums and parks. Nick loved Central Park, for he had freedom to explore, and Horace could help him perfect his knuckle ball. When Nick forgot to hold the ball in the correct position Horace tapped him on the head and said with humor, "Knucklehead." This word caused him to focus and the ball dipped and curved as it should. Horace concluded that lighthearted reminders and love were the best teaching methods, something he missed growing up.

John gave Nick $8.00 a day spending money on museum days. He had the option of spending it all at once or saving the money for a more expensive item. Nick, as a child of an alcoholic and one never certain about what tomorrow would bring, spent the entire amount on a daily basis. Since he received $1.00 for every birth year it would be an expensive proposition if he lived with them until he was twenty-one. Georgia wanted to show her nephew the world, the way they had with Val.

The Museum of Modern Art, MOMA, was a place of interest to the three adults, but Val thought Nick a little young to look at abstract art for very long. They decided to split up. Nick went with Rick (Nick enjoyed the name similarity and Horace felt Rick was less demeaning than Val's preferred Ricky). The two boys (Georgia felt that Horace had the maturity of a nine-year-old) decided to check out the design exhibit. Val and Kasey chose to begin at the top and take their time exploring all the floors. Nick suggested they meet at the gift shop. Everyone knew that meant take your time.

As the two girls reached the fourth floor of MOMA where still photography only was allowed, Val panned the room taking sequence multiple shots. She turned to capture a new angle and spied Kasey frozen in front of the Andrew Wyeth painting of *Christina's World*. It was considered his most famous work and psychology professors often used it for discussion. The image depicted a young woman crawling toward a distant farmhouse. Noticing the anxious expression on Kasey's face Val inquired, "Is everything okay?"

Kasey said, "I need to sit down." They moved to a quiet space where she confided, "I used to have a framed print of that in my room in Delaware. When Dad died, we had to sell everything to pay the hospital bills. Mom insisted I keep the one piece of art my father gave me as a memento." Thinking of her father's lingering bout with colon cancer caused her to weep. Val held her hand and they sat side by side until Kasey recovered.

"In our new home, I wanted to rip Christina out of the picture and turn her away from my stepfather's house in Pennsylvania. That's the way I felt when you picked me up. Christina could only crawl toward the house, but thankfully I could run from it and I did."

"But why? Was life so different after your father died?"

"It became a living nightmare. The night you picked me up I considered drowning myself in the reservoir to the left of the house. If I had turned in that direction I wouldn't be here today. Instead I turned right and ended up on the highway. I'm glad I did."

Val agreed. "The whole time I was growing up, I dreamed of having a sister. I'm thankful you took the right turn." They smiled affectionately at each other and hastened to the gift shop to meet the boys.

When they returned home, Val told her mother about Kasey's reaction to the Wyeth painting. Georgia resolved to free Kasey from the horror that drove her to the highway that rainy June night. As one trained in drama therapy, she knew that talking about one's problems helped a person heal. She decided to join them on their trip to the Museum of Natural History.

When they reached the museum, Nick pleaded with Horace and Val to photograph him in the Dinosaur Wing so they headed for the fourth floor. Kasey and Georgia begged off because the first floor had a gem exhibit and a variety of other enticements, including a coffee shop where they could sit and talk if they were inclined.

On their way to the Hall of Minerals, Kasey became terrified when she saw a reflection of a stocky, fair-haired man in the nearby coffee shop window. She grabbed Georgia's hand and dragged her out the exit door, saying, "It's Barry. He's found me. Don't let him see me. How did he find me?" Hysterical with fear, she pulled Georgia across the street to Central Park where she collapsed on a bench, checking behind her to see that they weren't followed.

Georgia attempted to calm her, "Kasey, it's OK. There's no one following us. No Barry just nannies with kids." She sat next to her, "I think it's time you told me what happened the night we took you in."

As tears streamed down Kasey's face she blurted out the embarrassing truth, "I was raped by my stepbrother, Barry."

Georgia moved closer. "Have you told anyone?"

Kasey shook her head. "No. Initially it wasn't penetration but he made me do…things, things I didn't want to do but was helpless to stop. I thought I saw him in the coffee shop. There was a short, stocky, light-haired man that looked just like him." She clasped Georgia's hand harder.

Georgia considered that Kasey might be having a baby. She looked at her with compassion. "Kasey, if you're pregnant, John and I will support you both emotionally and financially." Kasey looked up in horror. "Nothing like that, not that way. He was escalating, but" she softened her voice to an embarrassed whisper, "anal rape and just once. Was it my fault? He said I wanted it and led him on. If I did, I didn't mean to. I hated him."

"You must never think it is your fault. Rape is a method of control and Barry should be locked up. He'll just do it again." She noticed Kasey looking around in fear.

"Does he know where you are?"

Kasey shook her head, "No one knows where I am, not even my mother. Barry threatened to kill us both if I told anyone and so I ran to New York, an easy city to be lost in."

Georgia smiled. "Or found in. You do know that we're glad to be your safe house." She checked her watch, "We'd better go back. I imagine Nick's in the gift shop by now. We can talk more whenever you want but for now you'd better 'Put on a Happy Face'."

Kasey recognized the song title from *Bye, Bye, Birdie,* and smiled for Georgia made her feel protected.

They entered the museum gift shop as Nick showed off his newly purchased dinosaur kit. "Look, it's a Tyrannosaurs Rex, with glow in the dark paint. Rick promised to help me put it together." Horace beamed with happiness, grateful for the chance to be of importance to someone who needed him.

Chapter 12

Wrapped in a Ribbon and Tied in a Bow

One Tuesday, in late August, Nick, Kasey and Horace took the subway up to The Cloisters, the picturesque medieval monastery and gardens overlooking the Hudson. As Nick ran around with another boy his age, Horace told Kasey about his early life, hoping that she would trust him enough to confide in him the way she had to Val and Georgia. He hated to admit it but he was jealous. He eased into his story by telling her about his parents.

"My mother's first job was at the Empire Roller Dome in Crown Heights, Brooklyn. It was the perfect place for someone who wanted to find a husband."

Horace was unusually talkative. "We moved to New Jersey in the '60s because all the whites were leaving Brooklyn. Father left the house at 6:30 A.M. and returned home twelve hours later, expecting dinner on the table."

Kasey noticed he did not use any terms of endearment; it was Father, not Dad. It seemed clear there was a strain in their relationship.

He continued, "At dinner, Mom would tell Father of the day's activities of her three sons. Our sins would be elaborated upon, and Father would beat us according to our transgressions."

She laughed in disbelief. "I can't imagine you transgressing very far."

He tried to gain her sympathy, "Usually Vinnie's transgressions only drew a few licks of Father's folded belt. I was next in line, and since I refused to cry, Father beat me harder knowing that my youngest brother Christian, who was named after Jesus Christ, was not to be touched."

Kasey was horrified. "What was so special about him?"

He responded bitterly, "Mom expected him to be a priest, and as a future man of God she felt punishing him would bring a curse on the family."

Nick interrupted them. "I'm ready for something to eat, an ice cream?"

Kasey, grateful for his intrusion, looked at her watch. "Dinner is fairly soon and we need to hurry." She took Nick's hand, and they dashed for the subway. As they waited on the platform, she said to Horace, "That's why you were so upset at Georgia's treatment of Nick on the fourth."

He nodded as the subway roared into the station. It was too crowded to sit so he stood thinking about the difference between Georgia's brief but firm treatment of Nick during the stealing incident and Father's ongoing punishment of him. For the first time in three years he realized that he received more compassion and love (he supposed it was love) from the Shultze-Hogan family than he received the entire time he was growing up.

He began to feel sorry for himself and rationalized. Because he never knew a mother or father's love he was never successful in relationships. Nobody cared about him and that was why he was the way he was. His mind was on overload as he considered that the four women he had affairs with had all left him for someone with money.

He had spiraled downward on the ride home and found himself walking up the subway stairs behind Nick and Kasey, who were deep in animated conversation. He was so happy at The Cloisters. He loved watching Nick thrive in his new environment but now he was in what Val called his 'I'm gonna eat some worms' funk.

Nick ran up the townhouse steps followed by Kasey. Horace felt lonelier than ever. No one cared. He wasn't part of their world. He watched them go inside and envied them their happiness. In his misery he ran into the closed door that shut behind them. He tried the combination but was so upset that he couldn't remember the final number. He rang the bell in anger. Val opened the door, and everyone shouted, "Happy Birthday!"

As he entered the house, he was overwhelmed. Paper streamers hung from the chandelier, a decorated cake waited on the dining room table and, best of all, he smelled Chicken Saltimbocca. He looked around at their happy faces. He had forgotten, it was Tuesday, August 22nd, his 40th birthday. But his New York family remembered. They even cooked his favorite food. He beamed with happiness.

John handed him an antique book. "It just came into the Strand and I didn't have time to wrap it. It's by the writer and poet Bayard Taylor, the author Val said you went to research in Kennett Square. This is a first edition, written in

1870 called *Joseph and His Friend: A Story of Pennsylvania.* Val said it's about the friendship between poets Fitz-Greene Halleck and Joseph Rodman Drake."

Val's camera was whirring as she panned onto the book and then up to his face. He was overwhelmed and blurted out an abrupt, "Thank you; it means a lot. No one has ever given me such a present before."

Nick ran upstairs and returned with a wrapped book and handed it to Horace as he gave Val a wink. "Here's my present. Val and I bought the paper from the man at the 99-cent store." Everyone smiled, for he was so proud of his newfound honesty. "It's also a first edition. Val swore you would like it because you probably missed it when you were growing up."

Horace, as excited as a kid at getting another present, ripped off the paper to find Shel Silverstein's *Where the Sidewalk Ends.* He thanked Nick with a high five.

Georgia entered with the Chicken Saltimbocca as John pulled out his usual head of the table armchair and said with a flourish, "Here Horace, the place of honor for the birthday boy."

Kasey sat next to Horace and gave him a small wrapped gift, which he handled with care while flashing her a sincere smile. Her present was a journal to use for his writing ideas. He opened, it and lowered his head to hide the tears of happiness welling in his eyes. He examined the group photo that Val had taken of them on Georgia's birthday. He smiled at the memory, surveyed his New York family and knew that here was where he belonged.

Val grinned as she captured his glowing face. Through the lens, she saw a very happy, dark-haired, handsome man. She realized he could always be this good looking and decided to edit the frame into a photograph to hang on their wall of family memorabilia.

Horace's heart warmed as he looked around the table. It really had been a good day after all, and he decided he would spend the night reading from his new books. Perhaps he would focus on writing in his new journal. He wasn't in the mood for e-mails.

The phone rang. Val, who was nearest, answered and turned to Horace saying, "It's your mom. Probably calling to wish you a happy birthday."

Everyone got up, wanting to give him some privacy. As they carried their plates to the kitchen, Horace took the phone with a smile on his face,

"Hi Mom. We just finished eating. It's been a wonderful birthday."

His face fell as he realized she had not called him about his birthday at all. She was screaming about his brother, Christian, who was fired from his job in Florida and moving back home.

"That bastard baseball coach fired him last June for no reason. He has no job and his roommates have been floating his rent fur the past two months."

"Slow down, Mom. He was fired last June and never told you?"

"No, he was hoping to find another job so I wouldn't know. He always wanted to save me from worrying. He's such a loving son."

"Hasn't he done anything at all to bring in money?"

"He's a trained Phys. Ed teacher. What do you think he should do work at a fast food joint?"

"What about teaching at a Catholic School? Can't you or Father call up the area parochial schools? He won't need New Jersey certification for that."

"We did that. No one will hire him because he can't get a recommend. No one ever helps Christian."

"Mom, he needs to help himself. You and Father never disciplined him. I was beaten and forced to work when I was growing up. Christian never was."

"So now it's all my fault. You always blame me. Christian, God bless him, was supposed to be a priest. He's so well spoken; he has such confidence, despite the fact that he's only 5'6". And shortness is a handicap for a man. You're lucky; you're 6'1". You got the Gary Cooper dark-haired looks, and the taller height. If you love me you'll find him a job."

She had been crying and yelling the entire time, and Horace felt his happiness slipping away. He tried to reason with her, "It's August 22nd, Mom, too late to get a teaching job. Schools start too soon." Thinking quickly to stop her wailing, he told her, "Some of my acquaintances from Baruch work for the Marriott Hotel chain, and they may have openings." She was quiet. "He can live with you and commute in."

"I'll tell Christian that you'll get him a job by September." She hung up with no mention of his birthday. He looked around the empty room. The day ended badly, but he knew that someone was waiting in Australia.

Kasey and Val saw his dejected frame as he headed to his room. Val turned to Nick and said, "Come on, let's go across the street to the park for an hour.

"Let's get Rick. It's more fun if we four are together."

"I think he needs some time alone. After all he was with you and Kasey all day and with all of us so far tonight. C'mon."

The three headed to the playground.

Horace sat in his room waiting for his computer to open. He thought about his mother. He never understood why she didn't love him the way she did Christian. His daydreaming ended when his eyes shifted to the computer. His e-mail folder was empty. Just like his mother Emma had forgotten his birthday.

Chapter 13

Tradition

It was the Sunday before Labor Day, and John was sticking to the family tradition of taking the family to see a hit musical. Today he had chosen one of their favorites, *42nd Street*, the first successful stage musical ever made from a musical film.

As John walked downstairs, he looked at the empty living room knowing it would soon be crowded with college students and Nick's new friends. His thoughts were interrupted by Georgia, Horace and Kasey, all dressed to the nines. Val met them at the top of the stairs wearing tap shoes from her high school production of *Anything Goes*. Nick, wearing a sport coat and tie, breezed down the handrail shouting, "Look at those tapping feet!" He landed with a bump, took the familiar 'Ta Da' pose and raised his arms toward Val who tapped her way down the stairs. It was a picturesque moment, but since the photographer was part of the action John would have to hold the memory in his heart.

Val changed her tap shoes for flats and they walked the twenty blocks to the theatre. Nick loved the show right from the instant the curtain was partially raised to show the dancers' tapping feet. He nudged Val, who was seated to his right and they grinned. It was a show for all ages and the audience loved the escapism, the dancing and the romance. Everyone felt like tapping their way out the exit doors after the lengthy standing ovation for the performers and orchestra.

Val took Nick's hand, and they belted out the finale as they headed down Ninth Avenue. Kasey and Horace, wearing the new suit, shirt and tie that John purchased for him walked behind. Georgia pointed to his dark socks, which peeked out from the tops of his black shoes and they smiled. Horace was on his way to becoming a true man of the business world. It had been a fun afternoon and one to cherish.

Georgia told John she was going to take Nick to more matinees. "I'll start with Elton John's *Aida*. It's playing at the Palace, the old two-a-day vaudeville theatre that Dad loved. Maybe I'll run through a few of the old routines he taught me." Her creative energy took over as she continued, "I'll get Nick and Horace to perform the famous Abbott and Costello routine "Who's on First" at my next 'Gathering'."

Her imagination sped on, "I'll pick up the audio version at the Lincoln Center library for Nick. He'll love imitating Costello's whining inflection. Since reading helps Horace memorize, I'll have you move Rudy's framed copy of the comedy sketch to Horace's room." She envisioned her two adopted sons mimicking the routine that *Time* Magazine named the "Best Comedy Sketch of the 20th Century" and wondered if there was a video of the famous routine.

A few days later, John and Georgia stopped at the video store. Benny greeted them, holding a brown paper bag that obviously contained some VHS tapes. "Hi, they just came in but I didn't have time to wrap them for your anniversary."

John was thrilled; Georgia was puzzled, "What are they?" John handed Benny his credit card and gave the bag to Georgia who pulled out two Abbott and Costello videos, *One Night in the Tropics* and *The Naughty Nineties*. She kissed John and as he signed the credit card she told Benny, "This is great. Each one has a different version of 'Who's on First.' Nick will love it and Horace can't find any way of backing out now. Thanks for finding it."

Balding Benny was pleased to send two of his favorite customers away happy. They always included him in their events and were his only patrons that sat Shiva when his wife died.

As they began their walk to Grand Central, Georgia said, "This is better than a piece of jewelry." She looked at him with fondness. "You're a loving man, always a step ahead of me."

"I'm always three steps behind, but when you get obsessed with an idea I know there's no rest until it's accomplished. Besides, it made shopping for your anniversary present so much easier."

John and Georgia preferred low-key celebrations of their birthdays and anniversaries. Often continents, rehearsals, classes or other obligations separated them so they learned to celebrate every day they were together as a wonderful occasion. September 6, 2001 marked thirty years of commitment and since they were both home they took dinner at their favorite restaurant, The Oyster Bar at Grand Central. They walked uptown along Seventh Avenue and then across 42nd Street so they could view the Chrysler Building, their favorite skyscraper in the world. The temperature was in the upper 60s without a cloud in the sky. As usual, they held hands and talked about menu choices and wine selections. Georgia opted for strawberry shortcake, oyster Stew and halibut.

John was surprised, "No lobster?"

She answered, "Too messy for this dress. Remember the time Rudy came back from Japan and told the waitress 'In Tokyo they take my lobster out of the shell.' The waitress raised her eyebrows, smiled graciously and said…."

John finished her sentence, " 'For you, sir, we have the lazy man's special.' Your Dad was something else." They laughed at the memory.

"I still miss him."

"He was a generous man with wonderful stories, but you know he's waiting in your musical comedy heaven in the sky."

She smiled at the thought of her dad in his red sweater applauding Jimmy Durante, Milton Berle, Bob Hope, Fanny Brice and Ed Wynn. She loved musical theatre because there was a song to fit every situation and mood. She looked at John, who knew what she was thinking. They clasped hands more tightly as they headed into Grand Central to a very private celebration, oblivious to the noise and people that surrounded them.

Chapter 14

Somebody, Somewhere

Horace was excited. His professor at Baruch had hired him to teach a special topics course called *Research and Argumentation*. Usually adjunct professors were graduate students, but Horace's writing skills combined with his knowledge of financial research made him an acceptable candidate for the job. If he was diligent and got good teaching evaluations he might have additional classes in the second semester.

He was energized. At last, he was in charge of something. He went to his mailbox in the main office where he discovered that his recent poem was accepted for publication in the *Baruch Anthology*. This was a rhyming poem with a baseball theme. He wondered if Nick's birthday present of Shel Silverstein's book inspired him to branch out of his usual maudlin free verse and lighten up his writing style. As he left the building he noticed that the Mets were playing the Braves on September 21st. He had a unique thought, I'll treat everyone to a Mets game. I owe them so much and they root for me the way I do for the Mets. Maybe Mr. Flanders can get me discounted tickets.

Mr. Flanders got him discounted tickets and didn't mind reducing his editing hours so he had more time for his teaching preparation. Horace hurried to the Marriott focused on getting his brother a job as a waiter.

Georgia met her first semester students and explained to them why she gravitated to drama therapy over musical theatre, a subject she taught for many years in New Hampshire.

"I always loved theatre as a child. In later years, I was diagnosed with ADHD, which is why following me is sometimes like a roller coaster ride. If I get off track just bring me back by making a roller coaster motion." The class imitated her moving up-and-down hand and laughed. "I always questioned why people did things. My character studies were thorough. I remember the director of *Gypsy* where I played the stripper Mazeppa —" The class roared, "Okay, now you've all imagined me in that role, I'll continue. I wrote a ten page character analysis about Mazeppa's life as a child, where she was in the pecking order, her abuse, her need for love etc. etc. I picked up a dual degree in Drama and Sociology. Later I added in Psychology.

"After teaching musical and children's theatre for twenty some years, I found a home in drama therapy, helping clients find out who they were through role-playing in a safe space. This method is more immediate, which is liberating for the patients and satisfying for me. I hope you feel the same way at the end of the class."

Her smile grew larger as the class left the room talking in excited tones. Her home was always open to current and former students and she numbered her alumni as among her best friends. There was a common bond among them. She was grateful that John understood her love of being needed and even enjoyed the pandemonium that sometimes ensued. Val had grown up with student baby sitters and knew that she could always call on their enormous eclectic family for help.

Kasey finished her morning classes at the Borough of Manhattan Community College at Chambers and Washington Street. She loved spending time at St. Paul's Chapel a few blocks north of Trinity Episcopal Church, as it was the oldest public building in America and a peaceful place for thinking. She admired the large sycamore tree that shaded the chapel and wandered along, reading some of the old gravestones. Alexander Hamilton, the first Secretary of the Treasury under Washington, and his wife were buried there, as was Robert Fulton, the inventor of the steamship. She came across the grave of U.S. representative William Hogan, and wondered if John was a relation. She touched the gravestone with reverence, thinking, if I am going to die soon I'd be happy to have it happen here.

John was home packing for tomorrow's early morning trip to San Francisco where he was meeting Robert at the airport to pick up permanent guardianship papers for Nick. This would simplify things when it came to permission slips and other things that might be required during the school year. After a stopover in San Francisco he would fly to Tokyo and wasn't looking forward to the time change and jet lag. The extra consulting jobs meant he would be able to retire within a few years of Georgia and they could spend months on small river cruises and adventure travels. He would enjoy meeting people from different walks of life, not just her students.

Dinner was late because Horace wasn't there to cook the spaghetti, which his Italian heritage required be "al dente." John found himself tiring of Horace's mood changes and imagined he would have some depressing tale of injustice with which to mar his last evening at home. He was surprised when Horace ran in shouting and hurling his skinny, awkward body in the air as if he was Magic Johnson on the court. He yelled, "I got it! I got it!"

"Got what? What are you talking about?"

Horace responded in animated excitement, "I got a waiting job for Christian. He starts tomorrow at 6:00 A.M. at the Marriott. He'll complain about the early morning hour but it is a job at a very big conference and this is a great opportunity for him. If he works out, they will hire him as a full-time waiter."

Everyone was pleased. Finally, Horace could stop being "his brother's keeper." He fixed dinner and shared the good news of the day, his teaching assignment, his boss's kindness and the greatest surprise of all: his poem was being published in the *Baruch Journal*. He beamed with seldom seen happiness and said, "Since I owe all of you so much I arranged to get six tickets to the Mets vs. the Atlanta Braves on Friday, September 21st."

John reminded him, "I'll still be in Tokyo, so I hope you haven't paid for them."

Horace gulped. "I forgot," then he smiled a loving smile and looked at everyone. They were confused by his unusual vibrancy. "I know, I can giv——"

Georgia interrupted. "Don't you dare say Christian."

"No, my girlfriend, Emma, from Australia."

A surprised John said, "Australia! Did you meet her at school? A lot of Australians come to the states to upgrade their education." He frowned. "Or to find an American husband."

Val's interest was peaked. "Yes, Ricky," she reverted to the childish name, "where did you meet her?"

Horace choked on his wine and Nick patted him on the back. "I met her on the Internet." They were aghast. He hurried on, "But in the three months we have corresponded, I know everything about her. She writes so well about her education, her dream of becoming a Catholic, marrying me and having a large family. She is well traveled for she works at a tourist bureau. I know you will like her."

John hoped that things would work out for him, because Horace had no lasting relationships with women he met in person. "When is she coming to the States?"

"Definitely by Christmas, but she is trying for September. In December she will spend Christmas with me at my folks' house. If she likes New York, and me, she will get a job, and we will get married. She may be in Virginia for a short time in September so I am hopeful that she can train up to see the Mets game. That way I will meet her sooner, and she will meet all of you."

Georgia was suspicious. She and John, who travelled extensively, realized that the American passport was the best "aphrodisiac" in the world. They also knew that Australian language schools were filled with many girls from nearby Thailand who enrolled with the goal of marriage, citizenship, and after three years (to avoid deportation), a divorce. Once Australian citizenship was obtained it was relatively easy to obtain a US visa in search of a gullible American. She worried about him. Something she often did but she never wanted him to know, for fear it would lower his self-esteem even further.

Georgia knew students who had been duped by these foreign women romances but Horace seemed so hopeful that she poured wine all around as John filled Nick's glass with sparkling grape juice. Georgia raised her glass and toasted, "To a bright future for all of us, especially Nick's Rick." The name rhyme was a relief, and the clinking crystal created a happy sound that captured Horace's happiness almost as well as Val's whirring camera.

Chapter 15

Find Me A Hero

John's flight from Newark left at 8:00 A.M. That meant a 6:00 A.M. departure from 22nd Street. A private car picked him up at the house where Georgia, still in her summer bathrobe, kissed him goodbye. The driver placed John's luggage in the trunk and held the door open as John promised, "I'll call when I arrive in San Francisco, and again when I get to Tokyo."

Horace ran down the steps a few minutes later and hailed a cab for his first day of teaching at Baruch. He wanted to arrive early to post his office hours, check his roster and try to memorize his students' names before class began at 8:00 A.M. He offered to drop Kasey off at work. Knowing he was nervous, she agreed.

Val donned her tool belt, backpack and new leather converse. She planned a day of filming somewhere in the city. Georgia kissed her goodbye and said in Japanese, "Kio tsu ke te. Be careful. Remember, you're my favorite daughter."

Val rolled her eyes at Georgia's first day of school traditional comments and replied, "I'm your only daughter."

Georgia winked and said, "Then that makes you my favorite doesn't it?" Val laughed and waved goodbye as Georgia went upstairs to get Nick ready for school. He wanted to arrive early, which gave her time for an 8:00 A.M.

ice tea at the Moonstruck. She decided to take her laptop to Tekserve on 23rd Street. It was a beautiful morning for a walk, cooler than yesterday's 86 degrees. It was the perfect day to accomplish all the meaningless tasks that needed attention.

VAL'S STORY: At 8:46 A.M. a plane crashed into the north face of the North Tower of the World Trade Center. It looked to Val and her friends as if a commercial plane had gone off course and rammed into the building. Val wondered how that could have happened? Maybe the pilot had a heart attack, but what about the copilot or autopilot? Something was terribly wrong. She and her fellow-student filmmakers checked their positions to see if they could get four different views to be edited together.

Suddenly she heard a deafening roar. She panned her camera as a huge jetliner smashed into the second tower. It immediately became a giant fireball. She said, "Oh, my god. This is no accident. It's a planned attack."

Thinking of her mother and knowing she might be in a classroom, oblivious to the madness downtown, she pulled out her cell phone. There was no connection. She signaled her crew to keep filming as they moved further east away from the Towers.

Her lens caught mothers turning their children away from the buildings. She zoomed in and captured the horror of desperate people jumping to certain death. She and her crew shut off their cameras. Val told them to get to their families and safety. She grabbed her gear, saw long lines of people waiting for the pay phones, and decided to run uptown to Nick's school. She kept her cell phone in her hand, hoping Georgia would call.

Georgia, A New York Story

HORACE'S STORY: 9:20 A.M. Horace's class was over, and the students seemed to like him. They even laughed at one of his jokes. He was packing his briefcase in an invigorating and buoyant mood when he heard the news of the first plane.

He thought of Kasey somewhere down on Chambers Street. He knew her habit of spending free time at Trinity Church, across from the Towers, and he panicked. She didn't know the city very well and if she got disoriented she would get hurt. He rushed from his office and forgot his cell phone in his rush to find her.

He ran across 24th Street. If he was walking, it would take nearly one hour, but he ran to save her. He was wearing his black Italian, long-toed dress shoes meant for impressing, not running. The oversized shoes slowed his normal sneaker paced rate down but he continued to run as if entered in a marathon.

He spun right onto East 21st Street by Gramercy Park, and then down Park Avenue South and through a very crowded Union Square at 14th Street.

Twenty minutes later he turned onto Chambers Street and at first tried the deli where she worked, but he couldn't push his way through the crowd begging to use the landline. As his frustration built he screamed, "Kasey!" Colleen yelled back, "Trinity Churchyard or St. Paul's Chapel!"

It was nearing 10:00 when he reached St Paul's Chapel just as the South Tower imploded. Gray-white clouds filled the sky and moved down the street. It was 10:05. He coughed through the smoke; his feet slipped on the debris

84

from the towers. Where was she? He opened the door to the chapel to escape the smoke filling street and saw her among fifty others. She was praying and crying. He hugged her to him but she pulled away in terror. He said, "Kasey, it's me, Horace." She clutched him and they cried tears of relief.

GEORGIA'S STORY: 9:45 A.M. Georgia was on the building roof of the computer store where she and the tech staff watched the second tower implode. As a trained therapist she comforted them as best as she could and when they seemed relatively calm she went down to 23rd Street. As she exited the building she saw one of her former students, Pat Belmont.

Pat grabbed her and said in a shaking voice, "I was there. I was at the World Trade Center. I was late for work but when the train came into the station I could smell smoke and felt an overpowering urge to get away. A fellow passenger took my hand to protect me from getting knocked over and it took us at least forty minutes to get up to Union Square."

She continued and, as she relived the emotion, she picked up the pace even more. "I passed a man in a car with a radio blasting and asked him what was going on? He replied that a plane just hit the Pentagon. I looked at my watch. It was 9:37. The way he said it made me think he was joking. I said this is not a good day to be joking about something like that. He replied that he wasn't joking. I've got to go."

Georgia was in shock. This scenario might be playing out all over the country. She told Pat, "If you need a place to stay, let me know. We've plenty of room. And let me know how you are. I love you."

They hugged, wanting to cling to each other for much longer but neither could spare the time. "I love you too, Georgia."

As Georgia watched her go, she heard her cell phone ringing in her purse. It was from John who was probably delayed at Newark. Maybe all the New York airports were closed. Georgia moved to the quieter lobby of a store and answered. She listened in horror as she realized his plane was being hijacked.

"Honey, four men have just rushed the cockpit."

"Oh, my god."

"Are you, Val and Nick all right?"

"I'm on 23rd Street and haven't heard anything from Val. I imagine the teachers will keep Nick at school. Do they have guns? I don't understand. Why Newark? The planes that hit the Towers were from Boston, not New York. I just heard the Pentagon was hit."

"We're under attack. Someone is sure that our plane is headed for the Capitol and everyone voted to rush the cockpit. It will be a miracle if anyone gets out alive but we may stop a national disaster. I probably won't see you, Val, or Nick again but know that I love you."

Reality hit her, and Georgia began to sob, "I love you too, oh god, I love you so much. Please come home to me, please!" Suddenly, her phone went dead. Trying in vain to return the call she knew how empty her life would be without him, her support system and her rock. He was there when her parents died, when Val was born and when her students began dying of AIDS. Although she never saw him cry she knew he always shared her anguish. They loved the world they had created. Their married life, both in and out of the bedroom, was exciting and happy. They were of the same mind, the same value system. He was irreplaceable. She dialed again. The cell phone went to message.

She grasped a parking meter for support and cried. A total stranger reached out to her, "Is there anything I can do?"

She shook her head knowing that John was the only one who could ever help her through the rough spots in her life. He understood, as no one else ever would, her need to grieve alone and her ability to set sorrow aside as she looked to the needs of others. Tears streamed down her face as the reality of life without her best friend tore at her heart. Knowing that there was no time for her emotions she answered through her pain, "No, no, it will be all right. I'll be okay. My students need me." She looked at her watch. It was 10:03. She hurried south on the Avenue of the Americas, side-stepping the panicked people running north directly at her. Moving against the massive tide only strengthened her resolve to get downtown and she picked up her pace.

A sudden surge in the crowd caused her to lose her footing and she began to fall but was saved by the same stranger who offered his assistance on 23rd street. This time he pulled her to the safety of a doorway. She looked up, noticed that he wore a clerical collar and found renewed strength in the knowledge that someone was watching out for her. As she began to thank him the people around them grew silent and things seemed to be happening in slow motion. Everyone was looking west, toward the Hudson, and as the smoke cleared there was a united gasp of horror as each one absorbed the reality that the South Tower was no longer there. There was only an empty space.

It was 10:05. Georgia clung to her savior as they both felt the events of the morning crashing around them and cried in mutual anguish. After a few minutes, Georgia, drained of personal emotions, refocused her energy on the task of getting to NYU. As they hugged goodbye the rector told her, "I am at the Church of the Holy Apostles if you ever need someone to confide in." She nodded and gave a slight smile. He turned north as she moved south talking her way through the police barriers that denied entrance to those less determined.

THE AFTERMATH: Val was emotionally and physically exhausted as she entered the house with Nick, and saw the light blinking on the answering machine, she hit playback. As the machine rewound Georgia arrived home. Kasey and Horace followed.

The machine:

1. "Where d' hell are ya'? Der are thousands a' people down here…"

Val fast-forwarded.

2. "I hadda' wait in line for a pay phone. The fuckin' cell don' work. Shit. I'm callin' ma and tellin' her y' neva tried t' find me. Ya' piece a…."

Val hit erase. No one wanted any memories of Horace's garbage mouth brother.

Georgia, not ready to tell them about John, inquired about their days.

Kasey said, "Horace ran all the way from Baruch to save me. I was in St. Paul's Chapel, directly across from the Trade Towers. The chapel was saved from falling debris because everything fell on a hundred-year-old sycamore tree."

Val interjected, "I was filming right there and as I watched those trapped people trying to escape I knew that I was not cut out for any type of journalism that focused on human tragedy. I am devoting my cinematic life to recreation activities. I'll begin with Mom and Dad wedding pictures, and include my baby announcement, recital costumes, Nick on his first trip to New York, our trip on the Circle Line, Ricky's first year at our house, and end with our newest addition to the family, Kasey."

Georgia couldn't hold back any longer. She took a deep breath and began in a brave voice that soon cracked as her eyes filled with tears. "The memories are more important than ever Val."

Val grabbed her mother. "What's wrong?"

"Dad was on United Flight 93."

Val didn't make the connection. "Did he get re-routed when they shut down the airports?"

Georgia continued, "Flight 93 was the one the terrorists planned on flying into the Capitol or the White House. The passengers, hearing that the Trade Towers were hit by planes, decided to storm the cockpit and the plane crashed."

Horace added, "Twenty minutes from Washington."

Kasey started to cry, "We had no idea."

"I was so absorbed on filming that I didn't even hear the news." Realizing she would never see her father again, the pent up emotions of the day poured forth. She hugged her mother and they wept.

Nick started to cry, "I'll never see Uncle John again and he was such a good father to me."

Horace, experiencing the same sadness, hugged him. Kasey, reliving the pain of her own father's death, found some relief in holding Nick's small hand.

Georgia whispered to Val, "His final words were about loving us. He did what he had to do. God, I'll miss him so much. We had a bright future and in an instant it's all gone. The only thing holding me together right now is knowing I have you." Val hugged her mother more tightly.

Suddenly, bright lights shone on the house. Realizing the news media was searching out those inside, Horace, followed by Val, ran to make sure the door was locked but they were too late. Horace's egotistical brother, Christian, rushed in yelling, "I was nearly kilt down der y' stupid bastard." Val looked at him with hate and slapped him across the face saying, "We do not use that kind of language in this house and you won't either." Val turned to take Nick and Kasey upstairs where they could grieve in private.

Christian started to go after her, but when Horace grabbed his arm Christian turned on him. "Call Mom right away. She's ready t' kill y' fur gettin me that job down der."

Horace looked at Georgia for approval, for the call was a long-distance one. She nodded and busied herself in the dining area. Georgia was a delayed reactor who grieved inwardly, the way she had when her parents died. She survived by forcing herself to set aside personal tragedy and focus on helping others. Right now she was worried about Horace and listened to the one sided conversation he had with his mother.

"I am sorry Mom that I failed to anticipate the World Trade Towers were going to be hit by terrorists the first day of Christian's job. No one expected it—I apologize profusely—I realize the PATH is no longer operational except from midtown but Christian can return via boat to New Jersey–"

"I will ask." He turned in misery to Georgia for once again he had to take the responsibility for his lazy, complaining brother. His speech went from formal to informal as he pleaded, "Georgia is it okay if Christian stays in my room for a few nights? He won't be any trouble. May I please tell my mom he'll be with me?"

His eyes radiated so much hope and she was so overwhelmed with her own sorrow that she agreed and moved to the stairs. Holding the railing for support, she climbed to the lonely bedroom, knowing her life would go on but it would never be the same. On her dresser stood a framed 8x10 photo of her athletic husband, riding a jet ski. His hair was wind-blown and his brilliant smile pierced her heart. She tried to lift her morale by softly singing Jerry Herman's "Time Heals Everything." But she choked on the final lyrics, looked around the room and cried in heartbroken solitude.

Chapter 16

It's a Scandal, It's a Outrage

Two days later, schools were still closed and the networks continued broadcasting the horror over and over. Young children were terrified. Georgia took Nick with her to NYU. He spent most of his days working with college students who were helping other children that had lost loved ones.

Val, determined to solidify her senior thesis topic, met with leaders of senior citizen centers, arts organizations, veterans groups and event promoters. She was unwavering in her desire to film happy times.

Horace worked at his research job, and although Baruch was still closed, he used his free time with his students volunteering at various blood banks and assisting those in need.

Lena, Georgia's seventy-five-year-old, next-door neighbor, convinced Kasey to volunteer at the Episcopalian Church of the Holy Apostles soup kitchen. This diverse church on Ninth Avenue and 28th Street was a beacon of hope when many blamed all Muslims for the horror of September 11th.

Everyone in the house was out helping people so Christian was home alone. Still angry at Val's slap, he entered

93

her room intent on destroying her photography. He opened her dresser drawers, picked through her bookshelves and cursed aloud, "Damn, doesn't she keep scripts, videos, even a diary of ideas somewhere? Shit." His fury built as he left empty-handed. He realized she must have things stored elsewhere.

He entered Georgia's room, a treasure trove of art and jewelry. He moved to John's dresser. It overflowed with foreign coins, watches and rings. He spied a Rolex and said, "I'll pawn dis d' next time I need ready cash." He didn't know that John often got knockoff watches from Asia. The fake Rolex might be worth $25.00 tops. He spied a ruby ring and slipped it on his finger. He started to pocket it, but reconsidered and said, "Better not take dis, it's d' only one wid a stone and too easily missed." Instead he found a gold initial ring. "Ah, just d' ting, probably a present that bitch gave her husban'; she'll tink it wen' down wid d' plane." He pocketed it to wear when no one would notice. He checked the room to make sure Georgia wouldn't know anything had been touched and headed up the stairs.

Christian entered Nick's book and toy-filled room. He envied the eight-year-old. Christian's mother, who he hated, had filled his room with religious icons. She expected him to be a priest, which was laughable. Christian delighted in smashing a few of Nick's model airplanes but opened a window so it would appear that the wind knocked them off the window ledge. Satisfied, he left the room and headed across the hall.

He entered Kasey's room. He sniffed her clothes, breathing in her smell, and spent some time in the underwear drawer. Her desk was locked. He pulled out his switchblade and slid it into the lock. Click. He was in. Her school records from Wilmington, Delaware listed her as Kelly Christine Thompson, no mention of Kasey. He'd have to check that out. He heard the downstairs door open and relocked the desk so Kasey wouldn't notice her room had been violated. He decided to get out of the house. In the doorway he brushed lasciviously against a pretty college student and oozing sociopathic charm said, "Oh I'm so sorry. I'm still off balance because I was in the Marriott when the Tower pulverized it." He noticed her look of pity and smirked as he exited.

Later that evening, Pat was finishing up the story she was telling Georgia before the second tower fell. "I had to walk to my third job of the day. It was at a restaurant on Eighth Avenue and 56th Street."

Junie was astounded, "You walked all the way from 23rd to 56th?"

"Actually, much further. No one knew if Penn Station, the Port Authority or Times Square were targets. I braced myself for the safest walk, which forced me over to Tenth Avenue. My feet were killing me.

Georgia queried, "You were still in heels?"

"Yup, stupid planning on my part. Now I always wear sneakers to work and carry my shoes. I learned a valuable lesson that day."

Joel piped up, "Yup, be late for work, carry extra shoes, and (in his mother's voice), make sure your underwear is clean, just in case."

Many related to the underwear line because they had heard it many times from their own mothers.

Pat continued, "The blisters were building and my pace was slowing, but I got there. It took an hour. The other waitress loaned me an oversized pair of scuffs that got me through the night."

Teddy asked, "Were there any customers?"

"The place was packed 'til closing. No one wanted to be alone. Everyone needed to share stories or find out how others were coping."

Lena, the elderly neighbor who lived in the city her entire life, added with a strong New York accent, "If there's gonna be a tragedy there ain't nuttin' like a New Yorker to see ya' through. We're tough and hard-boiled but when the chips are down we always pull together. Believe me, there ain't no better place ta' live. Been in the neighborhood since the Depression and here I'll stay til I can't make it up the forty-five steps to my third-floor walk up.

The students were interested in the old, rent controlled, cold water flats they read about in novels but before they could ask any questions, Val rushed in with her camera, slamming the door behind her, "When are those people going to leave us alone? I finally started turning around and filming them. So disrespectful and annoying."

Teddy agreed, "The paparazzi are always somewhere they shouldn't be."

"From now on I am only filming parades, festivals and night life. I want to celebrate the good things in life.

Lena urged her on, "Honey, you go for it! It's something I'd watch. History in the makin', right here on 22nd Street. You can film us all at Clement Clarke Moore Park as I read, *A Visit From St, Nicholas,* on the last Sunday of advent."

Georgia was thrilled. "You're doing the reading this year? Congratulations."

Lena grinned her toothless grin. "Of course I'll wear my false teeth for the occasion."

Teddy began singing in his tenor voice, "We Need a Little Christmas." The others joined in.

Suddenly, Christian flung open the door and the fun ended. In an attempt to gain attention he invited the photographers to film the gathering. "I live here and what we went through was horrible. We're still grieving."

Georgia wasted no time in yanking him into the room and slamming the door behind him. There was dead silence as everyone watched.

She started speaking in crystal clear speech and perfect diction, which she only used when angry, and right now she was seething. She looked at him with disdain and said mockingly, "Christian, is it? Now that's an odd name for someone who has no Christ like compassion in his entire body. You need to go upstairs and get your things. You have exactly five minutes to get out of here."

An angry Christian moved toward her. "You sound just like my mother and she can be a real bitch."

Val stood, ready for a fight, but Kasey stopped her for she wanted to see how Georgia handled this pugnacious little man, who reminded her of Barry, her stepbrother, both in looks, size and crudeness.

Drawing herself up to her full 5'8" stature Georgia looked down her nose at him. "A bitch is a female dog or maybe *you* didn't know that. As she spoke, he backed away. "You did not suffer any losses during the World Trade Center attacks." He neared the bottom step.

"As soon as you knew you were safe you started phoning here and leaving abusive messages, filled with horrific language."

He fell onto the bottom step and heard people snickering.

Georgia continued humiliating him. "You should have known no one was here. We were all out helping people as you should have been."

She checked her watch and said with mocking sweetness, "You now have two minutes to get out and in case you have any ideas about striking back at anyone in this family, you can see that lots of people have our backs." She looked around with confidence at the eclectic family that filled the room. "You may find my support system incredibly eager to throw you out on your sorry ass."

Realizing he was outnumbered, the angry Christian turned and rushed upstairs, muttering under his breath. In less than two minutes he was down and out the door. As the door slammed behind him he heard applause and laughter. He swore revenge. "Ya' ain't heard the last of me, you stupid bitch."

Chapter 17

Take Me Out to the Ball Game

It was September 21st, and New Yorkers were focused on getting their lives back to normal. Today marked the first major sporting event since 9/11, and Horace was excited because he was acting as the head of the family and treating everyone to the game. He relished the feeling of importance it gave him. As he returned home from Baruch, he considered the parental love and support he missed as a boy and how much Georgia had changed his life. Once, during one of their many arguments, which she called *mental exercise*, she told him in no uncertain terms, "Horace, the worse thing I could ever say to you is I don't care." The fact that she had never said it renewed his belief that he was improving.

As he neared home he realized that he had often been close to saying those very words to his brother, but fear of his mother's reaction always stopped him. Horace suspected that much of Christian's meanness was due to the fact that he was probably molested at a young age. Whenever Horace tried to talk to Christian about it, he was cursed, and physical fights often occurred. He knew that Christian had difficulty with women, his drinking problem was worsening and his manner toward others was more abusive. Horace felt himself starting to cycle downward into one of his depressions but as he turned the corner his spirits lifted for he saw the family waiting on the curb and he ran toward them.

Val filmed them entering the limousine Georgia rented to take them to the stadium. She caught the excitement on Horace's face as he took his first limo ride. He was as thrilled as Nick as they entered Shea Stadium. Overall the crowd was relatively subdued because they were still recovering from their grief, but true New Yorkers always found ways to move on and Val and Georgia were no exception. They found comfort in being active and saved their grief for the privacy of their rooms and during the time they spent with each other.

Val focused her filming on Horace as they entered the stadium. Today he was in his glory for he often attended games there, usually by himself and always in the cheapest seats. Today was different. Mr. Flanders had gotten great seats and Horace relished in pointing out the stadium facts to Nick. "Shea is one of the few ball parks to always use natural grass." He wrinkled his nose in disgust. "Other parks use Astroturf."

Nick asked, "What's that?"

Horace, always a purist, answered, "That fake green stuff, like indoor-outdoor carpet. It feels scratchy on your feet and is bright green."

"That's what Mom put in our backyard so no one has to mow."

Horace was appalled and changed the subject. "See the foul lines?" He pointed; "They are one of the largest in the major leagues and it requires a really good fielder to catch the ball for an out. Most stadiums have less expansive outfields so the owners can fill the area with paying customers." They arrived at their seats. Horace sat between Kasey and Nick. Since Emma never made it to the States, Horace gave her ticket to Lena who loved baseball but hadn't been to a game in years. She confessed to being a Yankees fan but so was Mayor Giuliani, who was usually booed when attending a Mets game, but not today. As the "nation's mayor" walked onto the field, he was cheered for his dedication and tireless energy to a city in recovery. He was first and foremost a New Yorker and the fans loved him for it.

Diana Ross appeared with Liza Minnelli, and the crowd went wild. Liza, in a black sequined outfit, waved to her many fans as the opening to her signature song played. Nick asked, "Is that the girl from Oz?"

Lena answered, "No, that's her daughter. You're thinking of Judy Garland. I saw her act at Carnegie Hall. Now that was a great concert. Have you heard it?"

Nick shook his head and said, "At home we only have heavy metal stuff for my brothers."

Lena shuddered, "Yuk, too noisy, no focus on lyrics. What's the point? I have the album *Judy at Carnegie Hall*. I'll loan it to you if there's a record player at Georgia's."

Horace felt left out and said pretentiously, "I own the CD; you can borrow mine."

Liza belted out "New York, New York" as the crowd leapt to its feet. Men and women alike were crying with love and pride. It was a moment all in attendance would treasure.

The game began as New York healed by partaking in America's favorite sport. By the eighth inning the Braves were winning and Mets fans were glum. Nick thought of "Casey at the Bat" and wondered if he was in Mudville. A moment later, Mike Piazza stepped to the plate and hit a two-run homer, which brought cheers of enthusiasm from Mets and Braves fans alike. The crowd, the family and, especially, Horace went wild. Horace kissed everyone, even Lena and it didn't bother him that she forgot her teeth.

The stadium shook as 41,325 screaming fans and countless others, watching from their home TV sets, knew that Piazza's hit showed the world that although New York, like the Mets, had suffered losses, it would always come back.

The family went home happy. Nick clutched a Cracker Jack box tightly in his hand as Val videoed them leaving the stadium. Georgia realized that Horace had given them all a day to remember and with fondness watched him climb to his room on the fourth floor. At age forty, he understood, probably for the first time, how it felt to make a difference to those he loved.

Georgia looked in on a sleeping Nick, who experienced a day he would never forget and they had Horace to thank for it. She wished John was there to see how much Rick and Nick had grown and felt herself being overcome with a shortness of breath. Looking out Nick's open window she gazed up and found comfort in her belief that Rudy, Roberta and now John were cheering her on as she attempted to recover. Others looked to various religious beliefs for consolation but she found her strength from the unconditional love she received from her parents and John. Knowing they were watching over her gave her the necessary fortitude to keep going and she found herself smiling through her tears, knowing that she, her family and the city would heal from the tragedy known as 9/11.

Chapter 18

Tango Tragique

Georgia was helping Nick with his homework; Horace was cooking a pot roast. Kasey was setting the table for dinner and Val was emptying cassettes from her backpack when the phone rang. Horace answered.

"It's for you Georgia. It's Robert."

Georgia moved to the phone, thinking, two weeks later my insensitive brother wants to find out how Nick is holding up. She answered with a happy voice, "Hi Robert. We're fine here. I'm helping Nick with his homework; he's back in school, and we're just about to sit down to dinner. Three-hour time difference, you know." She lowered her voice to a whisper, "Did the divorce go through yet?"

Kasey and Horace eavesdropped, but watched to make sure Nick was focused on his homework and not listening to the conversation. There was a long silence and both watched Georgia's face changed from happy to incredulous. "What? You aren't going through with it? Are you crazy?"

Val looked up, as she knew her mother's anger was building. "You cannot be serious. There's no way you would lose the case. Have you no self-esteem or did it all go to me? What's the matter with you?"

Horace grabbed Nick's hand and took him to the kitchen, saying, "Come on, you need to give Kasey your surprise." Kasey worried about what was coming next. It was her birthday, and she didn't feel much like celebrating.

Nick returned carrying a lopsidedly decorated chocolate cake bearing nineteen candles. Georgia finished her phone call and listlessly joined the festivities. She didn't want to spoil the celebration, but she was upset with her brother and felt like crying when she looked at Nick. Val set up her camera "Remember, everyone, I'm only filming happy events." The adults went into their best acting mode, and the evening was a relative success. Horace and Nick went upstairs to read *Cigar of the Pharaohs*, the Tintin comic about Egypt, while Kasey and Val waited to hear the news.

"He wants him home. He says that Arrawika is so terrified of having him live in New York that she yells and cries every day. She hasn't changed her self-centered ways or her gambling habits and won't throw her sponging sons out. Once again Robert is enabling. Nick is going back to San Francisco tomorrow. My brother is out of my life forever. DNA does not a family make."

She sobbed in frustration. Val knew how much her mother was devoted to Nick and surviving the loss of two loved ones so close together was difficult, even for someone with Georgia's strength.

"What am I going to do? I can't take him to the airport; I'll be a basket case and he'll know something's wrong."

"Kasey, Horace and I can take him to the plane. After all, you have students who need you. Nick knows that."

Georgia nodded and left for her room where she cried herself to sleep, something she hadn't done since she was a little girl.

The next morning Horace took Nick's luggage to the cab as Georgia hugged him and said, "We New Yorkers are very tough."

He nodded and asked, "Do you think I'll be back in time to see the tree at Rockefeller Center and skate in Bryant Park?"

"That will be something to look forward to." Her voice caught in her throat.

Val, realizing her mother was about to crack, took him to the cab, saying, "Let's hope so. But I'll have to be the one to take you skating. Mom's a disaster on ice and roller skates. We don't want her to break a leg, do we?" She watched her mother turn back to the house. She brushed a tear from her eye, took a deep breath and saw Horace bow gallantly as he opened the car door for Nick, who gave him a heartless high five, and climbed in.

The four headed for Newark. Although the flight wasn't until noon the new rules required them to be at the airport by 9:00 A.M. In order to contain their emotions at parting Val and Kasey took turns reading the new rules for flying that would affect Nick.

Kasey started off, "Travelers must arrive at the airport at least three hours before a domestic flight and longer for international flights. At check-in, the FAA requires a photo ID, paper ticket or printed passenger receipt." Noticing Val crying, Kasey looked through Val's purse. "Here it is, the paper ticket your Dad messengered over and," she pointed to Nick's shirt and tickled him, "the photo ID? That's around your neck."

He giggled and looked at the photo, "It isn't a very handsome picture. Do I really look like that?"

Horace commented from the front, "Oh, much worse I would say."

Nick punched him in the arm.

Val, reining in her emotions, read, "Only passengers with boarding passes will be permitted beyond screening checkpoints. Boarding areas will be restricted to ticketed passengers only."

Horace and Kasey looked at each other, realizing that they wouldn't be able to see him to the departure lounge. Val held up the permission papers declaring, "They better let me go to the gate with these. After all, Nick is only eight. If I have to I'll pull a Georgia routine, and they'll have to let me in."

The cab stopped in front of the departure area, Horace paid the driver and checked Nick's bags curbside. The four headed inside. Nick smiled hesitantly for he was nervous about flying. Kasey reassured him, "It's safer now than ever. They have security guards to look out for you, and remember, you'll have lots of movies to choose from since you'll be flying first class. The flight attendants give you lots of attention because they're positive that you're very rich."

Nick reached into his pocket and pulled out a quarter, "I'm not rich."

Horace put up a brave front, for he knew everyone was counting on him. He opened his wallet and pretended he had no money either. He smiled at Nick and performed his only magic trick. He reached behind the boy's ear, saying, "Look, you do have money; you have five dollars."

Nick laughed and put the money in his pocket. Nick, realizing Rick was in anguish, reached into his ID envelope and slowly placed the treasured Tom Seaver baseball card in Horace's hand. He looked into his friend's moist eyes and said with difficulty, "Here, Rick, this belongs in New York. Will you keep it for me until I return?"

Horace was overcome with emotion, because he realized that Nick meant more to him than his once prized card. He yearned to hug the boy but didn't. He smiled bravely as they gave their 'cross my heart and hope to die' pledge.

After Nick and Val left, Kasey and Horace broke down in tears. After a few moments they talked. Kasey's anger was apparent, "What's wrong with Georgia's brother? Doesn't he care about his own son? How could he allow that woman to raise him?"

Horace, realizing the similarities between Georgia's brother and himself, spoke slowly, "Robert isn't a man of action. He has to think through every decision nine or ten times and even then he may not act upon his instincts."

"I never realized that you met Robert in person."

"Not in person, but I have talked to him on the phone when Georgia was not home. He always acted pleasant enough and I imagine he does not know what course of action is best. He seems to vacillate a lot."

Kasey shook her head in confusion because she came from a caring family who made decisions as a tightly knit unit. "I have no understanding of a parent who won't ask his own child what he wants. When I was his age my parents always asked my opinions and took my wishes into account. It's obvious Nick wants to stay here. Robert never even talked to him." Trying to lighten things she remembered her father, "No wonder dad always told me to 'marry an orphan'."

Horace was mired in his own thoughts. "I was raised by parents who never asked what I thought. Maybe that's why I'm a mess."

Kasey looked at him with encouragement. "Don't degrade yourself so much. You're a wonderful, kind-hearted man. But quite frankly, from the little I have witnessed, I am sorry to say that your family is 100% dysfunctional."

"Not me, you said I turned out all right."

She corrected him, knowing he didn't absorb the meaning of spoken language. "I never said you turned out all right. You have lots of problems, but your good points make up for some of them. Things can be overcome with good therapy."

He grew defensive, "I do not want to discuss my life with anyone. You have no right to be prying into my private affairs." His face grew red and he barked at her in anger for she was harping on therapy the way Georgia always did.

She lashed back, "Maybe long distance counseling is helping."

Horace felt his anger building. "How dare you go through my computer?"

She was horrified by his accusation. "I don't do things like that."

"Well someone has. I can tell it's been hacked."

Kasey was livid. "How dare you accuse me of prying into your private life? It's just that I hear you pacing around and pulling your computer chair in and out. Sometimes you don't calm down until 2:00 A.M."

Horace apologized, which was rare for him. "I am sorry. I'm just distressed about Nick. I am up late because I am having online discussions with my girlfriend from Australia. We have so much in common. You will meet her when she visits me at Christmas."

She was suspicious, "Did she ask you for money to buy her ticket?"

"Of course not, she has an excellent job with the Thai tourist bureau."

Kasey was confused. "Why would an Australian work for the Thai tourist bureau?"

"Actually, she is Thai by birth. She is studying English in New South Wales, and she married an Australian."

She was shocked. "Why are you e-mailing a married woman?"

"Her divorce just came through. She was married for three years and couldn't take his abuse any more. Apparently he beat her and accused her of running around with other men. She is such an innocent and her English is incredible. And, most important of all, she loves me."

Kasey was skeptical, "How many years does one have to be married to get Australian citizenship without being deported?"

"I – I do not know."

Kasey had read news articles about the burgeoning trend of foreign girls marrying and then divorcing Australians when they were past the time of deportation. These women eventually reached the USA. They 'tuk tukked', like those little motor conveyances, around the world searching for Mr. Rich, not Mr. Right.

Just as Kasey started to make him listen to the reality of his situation, Val returned wiping her eyes, "They made me leave him and he looked so sad. I wonder if we'll ever see him again? Arrawika just uses him as a way of controlling Robert and," she looked at Horace, "like some other men I know, he is an enabler."

Kasey, who was fed up with Horace's stupidity agreed. "I suppose until Nick becomes a juvenile delinquent like Arrawika's sons he will be stuck unnoticed in California."

Val needed cheering up. "Let's go home. I want to see what movies are playing on 23rd Street. Maybe there's a comedy or cartoon. We can grab brunch at the Moonstruck. Maybe Mom and Lena will meet us there."

It seemed like a good escape. Kasey was in agreement; "If I don't feel better after one movie I'm staying for a second."

Val said, "I may even opt for third. It's been a mean, sad day for us all." She ignored Horace who stood there reflexively, hoping to be included.

Chapter 19

The Gentleman Is a Dope

The months of September and October dragged by as the city and its inhabitants healed from September 11th. All in all, with Giuliani as mayor, things went fairly well. Val busied herself interviewing the elderly residents of Chelsea while Georgia spent more time with her students. Kasey and Horace, being more religious, found the Episcopal Church at the Holy Apostles helpful as they worked through their grief.

The church was only a few blocks from the house and they found that the shorter distance led to fewer arguments. Kasey was surprised at Georgia's refusal to give up on him and realized it was because her mentor considered him to be her "newest-oldest" student. She knew that Georgia never, ever gave up on anyone who had 'potential', but what she saw in Horace was "A Puzzlement" to Kasey.

One Sunday morning, as Kasey and Horace walked playfully through the fallen variegated colored leaves, Horace asked abruptly, "How did we save you that rainy night in Pennsylvania?"

Taken aback by his personal intrusion on her private life, she stopped and stared at him.

He said. "If you don't want to tell me you don't have to, but I won't tell anyone."

She decided to confide what had been the most brutal experience of her life. So many worse things had happened to so many others; at least she was alive. "This is something that I don't like thinking or talking about, but I have faith that you will keep this confidential. The night you saved me I was running from my stepbrother, Barry... He raped me."

Horace shoved his hands in his pockets and walked ahead in silent confusion. A hurt Kasey followed a few paces behind and they entered the church and took separate pews.

The word dirty crept into his mind as he knelt to pray. The sermon focused on Mary Magdalene and Horace knew he had no right to throw stones but thinking Kasey was no longer a virgin upset him and various visual images sullied his thoughts.

Horace often imagined that Christian, after counseling, would marry her but now it seemed that another of his dreams wasn't going to happen. He needed to ask Christian how he felt about marrying a victim of a rape. Naturally, he wouldn't mention Kasey's name, but he must know Christian's thoughts on the matter. He spent the remaining thirty minutes praying for guidance.

They walked home with an uncomfortable silence between them. Upon entering the house Horace went directly to his room. Seeing the pain on Kasey's face Georgia said, "C'mon, I'll make us some omelets. Ham, tomato and cheese ok?" Kasey nodded.

Georgia threw some butter into the skillet, "What's wrong?"

"When Horace asked what happened the night he and Val picked me up, I told him I was running from Barry."

Georgia cracked the eggs imaging the bowl was Horace's head, "What was his reaction?"

"He just walked away. He made me feel dirty."

Georgia's scrambled the eggs in the pan saying, "He had no right to treat you that way." She threw in the remaining ingredients.

"I thought he cared, the way he would if I was his sister but he looked at me as if I was a whore. Are you sure the rape wasn't my fault?"

Georgia put the omelet and some melon slices on the plate and handed her a fork. "Kasey, you were victimized. Horace has attended three years of monthly gatherings and that topic has been discussed more than once. He needs a wake up call and I know just when to do it." Kasey looked at Georgia's resolute face and wondered, "Where or When" it would happen. She couldn't wait to see him humiliated, and realized, with a twinge of guilt, that Horace had a talent for bringing out the worst in people.

Chapter 20

One Hallowe'en

Halloween arrived. It was normally a time for wild festivities and parades in the Village but this year was different. People were still recovering. Memorial services were ongoing and it reminded Georgia of the many she attended during the AIDS crisis and the loving quilt squares she sewed as a tribute to her former students and friends.

Over the past two months, she and Val had discussed the best way to honor John and they decided to each make a quilt square representing their fondest memories. "You are more artistic than I am," said Georgia to Val who responded, "You are more creative and knowledgeable."

Knowing that her intelligent daughter would soon surpass her, she replied, "I am a copy artist and like the old vaudevillians grandpa Rudy adored, I steal from the best, so I'll make my square after I see yours."

Val shook her head, "No way, we'll each do them in our own rooms and bring them out on Dad's birthday, April 24th. I'll pick out some fabrics for continuity. Maybe members of our eclectic family will want to add their own squares."

"It will be too big. I'd just like to keep it in the immediate family and hang them in a special place in our rooms."

Val thought back to the various Asian shrines she had seen and said, "Like in Japan." Georgia nodded. Their conversation was interrupted by the sounds of people gathering downstairs, for Georgia was having a Halloween open-house potluck 'Gathering'. Since John's death, the list had grown to include more neighbors and shopkeepers from the various International markets that surrounded them. The food was more varied and as they ate, they talked about New York, the changes in the neighborhood, and the annual last Sunday of Advent December celebration.

Lena filled them in, "On the last Sunday before Christmas, people of all faiths and persuasions gather in the park for the most famous annual poetry reading in New York. It's a diverse occasion that truly celebrates the meaning of peace on earth, good will to men. This year we need it more than ever."

Everyone missed Nick. The shopkeepers enjoyed watching him change from a sneaky kid they had to watch when he came in their store to one they loved talking to. When Benny asked her how she felt about her brother's removing him to San Francisco, Georgia responded, "I'm not ready to attack that monster in me yet, but maybe next time."

Sister Mary Paul, one of her current students yelled out, "*Cabaret.*"

Lena, who was an avid lover of musicals, both film and live versions, corrected her, "Sorry, Sister, the song title is "Maybe This Time" not maybe next time." She knew her shows.

Teddy, the tenor interjected, "Who cares? Let the fun begin."

And the Broadway lyrics game filled the rest of the evening. As everyone rose to leave, Georgia looked at Horace. He hadn't said one word and she was on him like a tigress.

"Wait everyone, Ricky over there has something to add."

The entire crowd looked in his direction as he tried to think of a song that might fit the occasion; the room grew silent. He became very nervous and began rubbing his head.

He whispered, "Home is where the Heart is."

"You know that doesn't count; it's an Elvis Presley song and not from a musical."

Horace knew she was disappointed in him for the way he treated Kasey. After an uncomfortable silence a song popped into his slow to respond brain. He said, "The Gentleman was a Dope." Everyone knew the title was wrong but it seemed to be an apology of sorts.

Georgia looked at him with coldness, "The Gentleman *is* a Dope." Horace nodded in agreement and breathed a sigh of relief.

As the house emptied the phone rang. Val answered. It was a long distance call for Horace, and the news wasn't good.

Horace grew pale as Christian informed him, "Ma had a stroke. She's in d' hospital."

"What caused a stroke? She didn't have high blood pressure.

Christian, as usual, turned on the blame game, "She's been upset ever since y' almos' got me killed by gettin dat job at d' Marriott. Her blood pressure was really high and she refused t' take her medication 'til you got me a job. There's nuttin' out here and I don' wanna live in d' city less I live wich you. Why don y' get a place of your own and we can room together, you could trust me t' pay my half a d' expenses. We could go t' ball games, an drink with yer buddies —"

"I thought we were talking about Mom's health. What did the doctors say? How bad is it?"

Christian continued his guilt trip, "Ma can't move her left arm or leg. She's in d' hospital and needs a bedpan. I don' wan' her home." He continued to whine. "I ain't changin' no smelly diapers and cookin' her meals. No way I'm emptyin' a peed in or pooped in bedpan. Dat's yer job. You're comin' home and takin' care a' us, damn it. We need y' now."

Horace didn't want to be needed in such a way. He was shaking in a mixture of anger and fear. Going home would mean the loss of his future at Baruch and he wasn't going to do it. For the first time in thirty-five years, he stood up to Christian.

He rubbed his head in agitation and said, "I am not coming home until the weekend. Mom can go to the local Rehabilitation & Health Care Center. It is near the house and you can stay with her all day to make sure she follows therapy instructions."

Christian whined, "Shit, I ain' spendin' all day wid her, getting' Dad's meals and cleanin' d' house. It's yer fuckin' job not mine. I don' cook; you were d' one she taught t' do dat female crap. Be here tomorrow." He hung up certain Horace would arrive as directed.

Horace slammed down the phone. Val, who was putting away her camera said, "What's wrong?" Kasey looked worried as well.

They were concerned about him; they cared. That moved him more emotionally than the news about his mother's health. "Christian needs me at home to take care of Father. Mom had a stroke. He says it's my fault she's in the hospital because she refused to take her medication until I found him a job."

Val was livid, "She's his mother too. Christian can take care of your mother just as well as you can and don't you dare feel guilty. If he weren't such a lazy bum, he would find his own job. You need to face the fact that your brother is an asshole. If you keep enabling him, he'll be leeching off you forever. What is he thirty-five? Horace, it is time to get him out of your life."

Kasey refocused the conversation. "Was her speech affected?"

He shook his head, "No, she has no use of her left hand or leg. But she can feed herself with her right hand and she can talk."

Val muttered under her breath, "That's too bad."

"Christian needs me home to take care of Father. Mom raised me to be the caregiver. I guess you could say I was more of a servant than a son. I was punished Christian was not. He was supposed to join the church as a priest."

Val thought that was a great idea. "Why doesn't he do that, and then you'll be off the hook; but god help the parish that has him as a priest." Her anger at Horace's inability to act was building.

Kasey asked, "What are you going to do? You're lucky to have your research job. Lots of people in the financial district were laid off after the attacks. Your teaching job holds such promise. It may mean two classes next semester and your poem is being published by the school literary journal. You are on your way to respectability as a teacher and writer. You can't let this set you back."

He looked at her and a manipulative thought flashed through his brain. "Your school hasn't reopened yet, and Colleen can give you some time off, do you think you can take care of Father for a few weeks?

Georgia, returning from seeing everybody off, heard the end of the conversation. She was appalled. "How can you ask Kasey to live in the same house with your father and that slimy brother of yours?" She looked at him with repugnance. "Your behavior is untenable! You are a selfish manipulative user of people, and I have had enough of it. Your dysfunctional family has caused us enough problems." She stared at him and held up two fingers, which she drew close to each other. "I am this close to throwing you out like the garbage you have become." She stormed up the stairs. Val ran behind. She had never seen her mother so unforgiving of this man she treated as a son.

Kasey and Horace sat in silence. His face resembled a droopy basset hound. Georgia was right about him but Kasey felt pity. He needed her, and he had saved her, more than once. She looked at him with sympathy and said, "I will help you as you twice helped me. I'll go to New Jersey and take care of your dad."

Horace felt his lip quivering with emotion. He lowered his head for he had no idea what to say. He treated her badly when she told him about her rape, but he was a man who rarely said thank you to a woman and so he sat there in a tongue-tied stupor.

Meanwhile, in Georgia's room Val was trying to calm her mother who had spent the last few minutes venting her frustration and anger. "Mom, you're upset because he reminds you of Uncle Robert."

Her mother was still furious, "That man is the most insensitive exploiter of people I have ever encountered. He deserves every conniving woman he gets. Maybe he'll learn a lesson when he meets this Thai e-mailer in person. He is a selfish, insensitive clot and I think it is time to get him and his smarmy brother out of our lives."

Val, knowing that Georgia's venting was her coping technique tried to calm her. "It's true, most of the time he philosophizes and prattles on nonsensically, but he usually means well. His problem is that isn't honest with himself and lies to cover up his inadequacies. He says one thing one day and a day later, he contradicts himself. C'mon Mom, you know that if we put our minds together, we can think of way to stop his exploitive behavior and wean Kasey of her need to be needed."

Georgia still felt an overwhelming urge to get Horace out of their lives forever but she looked at John's Jet Ski picture, which calmed her, and acknowledged that Val was right. They each tried to think of a way to salvage a bad situation for Horace and Kasey.

Val came up with an intriguing idea. Her eyes sparkled with delight as she said, "Let's have Horace's father come here. He can have Nick's room. That way Kasey won't have to be in New Jersey, and we can meet Father." Their eyes connected with glee.

Georgia agreed. "That works for me. I just hope the father's not like that slob of a brother."

Val opened the door and announced to Horace, "Since you are *still* a member of our family, your father may live in Nick's room. We'll pick him up this weekend and bring him home."

Horace felt like crying until Georgia nipped any sentimentality by saying in controlled anger. "You better cook meals we like and be on time to prepare them! I trust your father is nicer than your mother or brother because they didn't leave a good impression on this family. Goodnight." She turned into her room and slammed the door thinking, Dad was right, there *are* more horses asses in the world than horses.

Chapter 21

Fathers and Sons

Horace spun into Princeton Commons, a subdivision of new homes for seniors. As they turned onto Benjamin Franklin Drive, Val and Kasey saw a small, yellow ranch home that backed onto a beautiful wooded rear yard. To the side was a lovely fall garden filled with chrysanthemums, marigolds, some squash, a few Italian tomatoes, and some fall crocus.

As the car skidded into the rain soaked driveway, a thin, dark-haired man who resembled Horace greeted them. He wore a bright blue sweater, leaned on a cane and smiled. Horace looked uncomfortable but as Val and Kasey stepped from the car, Al shuffled down to greet them and shook their hands. Val pulled out her camera and began videoing. But first she asked, "You don't mind, do you?"

He chuckled and his blue eyes sparkled, "Not a bit young lady, I just hope this mug doesn't break your camera. You must be Val, which makes you Kasey." They nodded with pleasure. Horace stayed in the car. "Look, I even painted a pumpkin as a present for each of you." He pointed to the porch behind him and sure enough there were two decorated pumpkins. One was painted with red hair, freckles and hazel eyes and the other sported a blonde wig with a small cardboard camera at its base. The girls laughed. Horace frowned. He had never seen Father in a sillier mood.

Val put the pumpkins and Al's suitcase in the Subaru and climbed in. Horace peeled rubber and they headed for New York.

On Monday Horace left for work early, angry that everyone in the house was enamored of his father. He spent most of Sunday e-mailing and working on handouts highlighting the various argumentation examples from the film *Twelve Angry Men*. The only time he came out of seclusion was to prepare dinner. It was obvious he hated his father but the three women found Al to be a delightful resource and excellent storyteller, which is why Val wanted to film him for the oral history portion of her thesis.

Veterans Day was approaching and Val planned on interspersing elements of the annual Fifth Avenue parade with Al's stories. She sat Al in Grandpa Rudy's antique 1940s, arm chair (with matching footstool) and focused her camera. Kasey was continuing her interview about his return to America after the Korean conflict.

Val said, "Rolling," and started with a wide shot.

Kasey picked up where she left off. "You were telling about your wife's first job."

"Oh, yeah." Al remembered where he was in the story. "The Empire Roller Dome was the perfect place for someone who wanted to find a husband. We met in 1957. I was thirty-one, damn short, and a bachelor. I was back from eleven years in Japan. Rosemary thought I was rich. She always asked me to skate at the end of her shift. I walked her home, shook her properly gloved hand and left her at her home.

126

Kasey looked at him with a smile of puzzlement. "No kissing goodnight? No making out in the park?"

Al shook his head. A strange expression crossed his face that Val captured on her camera. The expression quickly faded. "Her favorite dates were at the famous 1,900 seat Ridgewood Movie Theatre in Queens. There we held hands, she rested her head on my shoulder, and asked me to marry her. I was twelve years older but lacked experience with women. Rosemary wanted a man she could control, and I fit the bill."

Val fixed her camera on both Al and Kasey's faces.

He continued, "We honeymooned in Niagara Falls and it was a disaster. She thought sex was like in the movies; a kiss good night and boom blackout. How the hell she thought babies were made, I don't know. Probably she believed in that stork crap. Sorry. At the end of the first try, she told me, 'Now I know how rape feels.' "

Noticing Kasey's discomfort, Val turned off the camera. "I think that's enough until Mom gets home. We'll grab a bite at the Moonstruck and show you the neighborhood."

They slipped on their hats and coats and headed to 23rd and Ninth. Val left her camera home. She wanted to take notes for Al's person-to-person narrative. She asked, "Why does Ricky call you Father and not Dad or Pop?

"Ricky! Hot damn!" He slapped his hand on the table and laughed loudly. "I should have called him that when he was growing up. Imagine living up to a snobby name like

Horace. Ain't no wonder that he's such a fuss-budget."

Val and Kasey looked at each other as their sodas came thinking maybe if Horace Ricardo Tedesco was a Rick to himself he would be a more relaxed, less melancholy individual.

Al continued with a sad aura, "Your Ricky is in fear of me when the one he ought to fear is that woman slobbering down her food in the rehab center. She made me do things to him that I'm ashamed of." His Eggs Benedict arrived, and elbow glued to the table, he hunched over and began to "inhale" his food. He chewed with his mouth open and talked at the same time. "I haven't had anything this good since 1957 when Rosemary took over my life and mandated what I could and could not eat. This is a treat. Should I go on?"

The girls' Cobb salads arrived which gave them something to focus on other than Al's spewing food. They nodded. He continued, "Our first son, Vinnie, was born nine months after our honeymoon. We moved to New Jersey in a small house near the train station so I could commute to the city. A few years later, we had a girl that was stillborn. Of course Rosemary blamed me for not being there to take her to the hospital. I was working damn it. Who knows when a baby is going to be born? She waited for a neighbor to come and take care of Vinnie and it was too late by the time she got to the emergency room."

"I'm so sorry, murmured Kasey, "it must have been terrifying for her."

Val agreed, thinking of the loss of her own father, "I can't begin to imagine the loss of a child. It's bad enough losing a parent."

Al remembered her recent tragedy and apologized. "Sorry, I'm stupid for bringing it up."

Val urged him to continue. "No, it's okay. I can't shut out people's stories because of what I've been through, please go on."

Al finished his food and was slurping coffee while he waited for his chocolate cream pie to arrive. He continued. "After that she had two miscarriages and then we had Horace. She was furious that he wasn't a girl so she tried to make him into one. She taught him to cook, clean and obey. To escape, he would feign sickness, stay in his room and read."

Kasey and Val now understood why Horace wanted to be a writer. One must be alone to write and Horace was usually alone. But neither understood how he could write about the human experience because he had no true or lasting relationships.

Al said, "Five years after Horace was born we had Christian." Whip cream poured from his mouth. He shook his head. She named him after Jesus Christ. We never had sex after that. She was thirty. I was forty-two." Val paid the bill and they left in private thought.

They stopped for a short rest in the park. Al liked seeing the diversity of the street but especially enjoyed meeting Lena and hearing her New York stories. As the longest living resident on the block she had survived the slum era before the gays discovered Chelsea. She had witnessed drunk, homophobic hoods beating up gay men, and physically entered many a fray with raised cane, screaming in her loud voice that scared off the toughs. She was a beloved and well-known New York character who was a regular at Studio 54 and various discos, when they were still around. Al and she swapped stories of their youth because each had grown up in Brooklyn. She and her recently deceased husband had moved to Chelsea when rents were cheap and stayed in the city she called "the greatest in the world."

The streetlights came on. Val spied Horace rushing down the street with his hands in the pockets of his wool pea coat. She yelled, "Hey hatless we're here." He started over but saw his father, spun around, and entered the house. Kasey, Val, and Lena looked at Al who shook his head. "I've got a lot of work to do before he forgives me."

They said goodbye to Lena and headed home.

After supper Val filmed Georgia showing Al various art work from Korea and Japan. Horace and Kasey were in the kitchen cleaning up from dinner. Horace pretended not to listen but Kasey found the stories interesting and opened the door. Georgia, knowing Al was in Japan during the occupation queried, "What branch of the service were you in and why did you join? World War II was over.

"I was in the Air Force. I joined to prove I was a man because it was hard to get in. So from 1946 until 1957, I was stationed in Seoul, Tokyo and Manila, and thinking about a military career. I never saw any fighting. Well at least not the military kind." His face was pained as he reflected.

Georgia was curious. "Why didn't you stay in the Air Force and become a career soldier? You were there for over ten years."

"I hit an officer and called him the "N" word. All my prejudices against anyone who wasn't white came out during the years I was overseas. I had been written up before and the men in my unit didn't like me. I was just like Christian, cocky, short, wise-ass, unappreciative and angry. I thought I was better than I was.

"I returned to the states, met Rosemary, and we were wed. I never felt comfortable around women and probably never should have married, but in those days it was expected. When Rosemary asked me to tie the knot, I hoped things would work out. But we never loved each other. I botched it raising my boys."

"What makes you feel that way?"

"I was gone from the house twelve-hours-a-day, even worked some Saturdays. When I got home Rosemary badgered me about how bad the boys were. She fired up my anger and I took out my sexual frustration towards her on Horace who never fought back."

Kasey, embarrassed by the subject matter but furious at his treatment of a young boy, admonished him, "That was an awful thing to do to anyone Mr. Tedesco, especially a small child."

Al looked grim. "Mr. Tedesco, ehh? No more friendly Al? I deserved that. Rosemary wouldn't let me hit Christian, because he was going to be a priest. A ridiculous idea. Vinnie was tough. He joined the military when he was eighteen and hasn't been home for twenty-four years. A phone call to me now and then, but he doesn't want anything to do with his mother. Right now, he's somewhere between Diego Garcia Island and Afghanistan. As a kid, he was fearless; I would chase him around the room to get a few licks in. He made me laugh, so I gave up.

"Horace was another story. He just stood there, bent over and pulled down his pants as I doubled my belt and whacked him until he yelled loud enough for Rosemary to hear. Then she would come in and tell me to stop. I followed her whipping demands because the lying bitch always promised a bedtime reward. For more than thirty-five years I fell asleep waiting for her unfulfilled promises."

Georgia looked at Al with pity, remembering the love her parents shared. Al felt shame. "I need to tell Horace I'm sorry but he won't talk to me. He blames me, and he hates me."

Georgia saw his rising emotions as he continued, "By beating Horace I felt intellectually and physically superior. As he grew to 6'1", I still beat him to prove to myself I was a man." He lowered his head, and his speech became strained at the thought of the meanness he had dealt his son. "Imagine a grown man beating his pathetic son just to feel better about himself?" Al started to cry.

Kasey and Val left the room. Georgia picked up a box of tissues, sat on the footstool and took his gnarled hand in hers.

After a few minutes, he quieted, took a tissue and blew his nose. They sat in silence, surveying the room, looking at the various Japanese Hiroshige and Hokusai woodblock prints and thinking. Georgia remembered the good times in her life; Al remembered the empty meanness of his. After a while, he squeezed her hand, "Thank you. So many wrongs, so much bottled up."

Although Al had bared his conscience it was clear the weight had not lifted from his shoulders and until he opened up to Horace the guilt would remain. Both father and son needed so much healing. Georgia knew she couldn't help either of them until Horace was ready to acknowledge that he needed therapy. She hoped he could close the wounds while his father was still alive.

Georgia respected Al. It wasn't easy for a man of his age and background to admit his flaws. As she turned off the living room lights she knew Horace was pondering in the dimness of the kitchen, the room he liked best.

Chapter 22

Ding Dong, the Witch Is Dead

Horace, upset that the women were fond of his father, insisted they meet his mother. Georgia refused. "Absolutely not." Val and Kasey, curious to meet the woman they called "witch," accompanied him. As Horace sped onto the turnpike he defended his hatred of his father, "How could you like him? He was the one who beat me with his belt at any minor infraction. Mom never hit me."

Val tried to get him to think. "You were in the kitchen listening. She manipulated him by withholding sex and lied about your misdeeds in order to satisfy her frustration that you weren't a girl."

Horace denied the accusation. "That's not true!" He left the car at valet parking and they entered the rehab center. The three reached Rosemary's room. Horace peeked in, "Hi Mom." He was upset to see his mother full of tubes and shuddered. He hated the smell of medical facilities and hadn't realized things were this bad. As he walked over to give her a kiss she began berating him, "It's about time you showed up. Poor Christian, he had to take care of me while you played in the city, you ungrateful bastard."

Val was in the hallway, snapping pictures of the nurses, but Horace thought by bringing Kasey into the room, his mother might show some crumb of gratitude. "Mom, this is Kasey. She has been spending time with Father while you are in here. Kasey, meet my Mom."

Kasey was polite; "Hello, Mrs. Tedesco. I hope you're soon back home." She smiled, but the old woman just grunted. Meanwhile, a desperate Horace dragged Val into the room. "This is Val. Dad's staying at her home."

Rosemary turned on him. "I don't care anything about that bastard husband of mine. I care about Christian, and you should too. You should be in New Jersey taking care of him. After all, because of you we all suffered."

Horace was confused. "What are you talking about?"

His mother looked at him with hatred in her eyes, "I had to take one entire month out of my life to nurse you both back to health. You were fourteen when you got the mumps. I was stuck home with you for two weeks, and then poor Christian got them. I was so relieved when the doctor said Christian would be fine because it wouldn't affect a nine-year-old the way it would a fourteen-year-old."

The girls were puzzled. Horace looked extremely uncomfortable.

His mother continued, "I knew when I saw what happened, I would never have any granddaughters from you. The doctor called it testicular atrophy and made it clear that you could have a loss of function. I knew when you married that your wife had no idea what she was going to find." She cackled. "That marriage didn't last long; did it?"

Kasey felt the bile rising in her throat and hurried from the room saying, "This is a private matter."

135

Val, in a fury asked, "Why didn't you get him vaccinated? They had shots for mumps back then. You're the one at fault. You got some real problems lady."

Horace was aghast. No one talked back to his mother. The harpy responded, "Let me tell you, you little slut," she said as drool ran down the left side of her face, "you won't be spending much time in bed with him when you get a look at what he's got, or hasn't got for a package. No present there."

Horace tried to usher Val from the room, but she broke free and faced the old woman in anger. "You're the cause of his problems. You forced Al to beat him because you're an angry witch who couldn't get what you wanted from life so you took it out on Horace. You're the reason the boys at school called him a fag, and a homo, and you laughed when you heard that Vinnie pulled down his pants outside the soccer shower and pointed at his malformation."

Horace gasped, "How did you know that?"

Val was quick to answer, "Your father and I talk a lot. You and he have a lot to discuss to end the animosity caused by that woman who made both your lives miserable."

Mrs. Tedesco began to gasp and tried to get out of bed. Horace rang for a nurse, who gave her a shot and called for physical restraints. The nurse confided, "She's had little strokes and angry fits all week. Refusing to go to therapy, being abusive to all of us. The doctors prescribed heavy sedation to calm her. But you will need to sign directives regarding extraordinary measures that you want to take. She named you as the decision-maker in her medical power of health care form."

136

"But Christian should do that; he's her favorite son."

"She insisted it be you. She could have named someone as an alternate but she only named you."

Horace turned to Val in triumph. "Finally, an act of affection. My mother loves me after all."

Val looked at him in disgust and tried to give him a reality check. "Don't you understand her game plan? By giving you sole power over her health she controls you for the rest of your life. No matter what you do you'll always think you did the wrong thing. It's sadistic."

Horace refused to admit that any woman was right when it came to his mother. He hurled the valet parking ticket at her and yelled, "Go back to New York and take Kasey with you. I don't want either of your opinions on matters that don't concern you. I'll stay in New Jersey and commute. Mom needs me." His mother grinned with malevolence as drool poured from her mouth.

Horace stayed by his mother's bedside, hoping she would tell him she loved him; but it wasn't until Christian arrived that she mentioned the word 'love', and it wasn't addressed to him. Christian only stayed five minutes; he didn't want to leave his buddies waiting at the bar without him. Rosemary had several more seizures that scared Horace. She was currently hooked up to life support, which his power of attorney gave him the responsibility of keeping on or turning off.

Horace was in a state of confusion, for he was in a situation that his religion or upbringing had not prepared him to address. He felt that removing the tubes from his mother would mean was killing her, and he knew he couldn't live with himself if he killed his mother. He began to panic and gasp for air. He didn't know what to do or who to turn to, and he felt abandoned by everyone. He needed to talk to someone, and knew it had been a mistake to send Val away, for she had helped Georgia when grandma Roberta died. He ran to the chapel and prayed for guidance.

When Val and Kasey returned home they told Georgia and Al what happened. Georgia suggested that Al call his parish priest, which he did before heading to New Jersey himself.

Father Joe found Horace in the chapel, alternating between crying and praying. He knelt next to him and suggested they go to the cafeteria, knowing that Horace would be less emotional in a room filled with people. As they ordered coffee, Father Joe began by imparting a little known fact. "Horace, I want you to know every priest in our order has a living will."

Horace was shocked. "But you are men of God."

"Exactly. The order believes there is a time for living and a time for dying. We don't want extraordinary measures taken to keep us alive, no feeding tubes or last minute operations, just pain medication so we can die in comfort. We've made our peace with God and lived a virtuous life. You mustn't feel guilty about freeing your mother from her pain. We believe that worthy people go to a better life.

Horace absorbed his words, but was unable to let his mother die without telling him she loved him. He rationalized. "Father, people come back from strokes all the time. Besides, Vinnie will want to come back from

138

Afghanistan to say goodbye. We'll need to wait for that. Maybe she'll come around once she knows he is on his way to see her."

Father Joe knew that Vinnie never wanted to see his mother again, and he suspected that Horace knew it as well but was using any reason to keep from making the final decision. He told him. "I've issued the last rites. Your mother has confessed her sins and is ready to meet her maker. Horace, it's time to let her go."

Horace rushed to his mother's bedside, and fell to his knees, crying and praying. He held her cold hand so she would know he was with her. She had always been cold to him emotionally and physically and he dreaded letting her go because once she was dead he would never know why she didn't love him. He looked at Father Joe in desperation but the priest made the sign of the cross. Admitting there was no hope, Horace reluctantly signaled the nurse that he was ready to let his mother go to heaven.

Father Joe contacted Al and stayed with Horace until Al arrived to find his grieving son sitting in the chapel before the stained-glassed window of Mary. He joined his son and the two sat in silence. After a few minutes Horace acknowledged his father with a slight nod. Al put his hand around his son's shoulder, and Horace sobbed, not for his mother's loss but because he realized, for the first time in his life, that his father cared about him. He felt a little bit of the wall of hate lowering as he helped his dad make the burial arrangements.

Chapter 23

Gone, Gone, Gone

They called at a nearby funeral home. When the funeral director introduced himself, Al surprised them all by sharing his lifelong dream. "I've always wanted a mausoleum with our family name on it as a memorial to the fact that we lived on this earth. It's going to take up less space in the long run and my sons will never have families so we might as well be buried together."

Horace was angry at the assumption that he would never have children, but then he had not told his father about Emma and her Christmas visit. He thought, wait until December and smiled smugly.

The funeral director beamed and opened a brochure filled with various types of mausoleums. "How many persons do you plan on interring?" Al thought a minute and counted off the names on his fingers, "Let's see, there's me, Christian, Vinnie, Pegeen (she was buried over there as a baby, but she can be moved), and Ricky here." Horace looked up in shock as Al winked and continued, "Who am I missing? Oh yeah, my wife." He chuckled. "It's a relief to forget her. That's six. How much is a mausoleum for six?"

The funeral director pulled out his calculator, typed in some numbers and announced, "Six persons will be $25,555. That amount includes the tax. But if you want a walk-in, then the price is $70,755 (tax also included), cash or bank authorized check."

Al was pleased. "I want the walk-in, even though the cost will wipe out my savings. I won't live much longer and my sons can split the money from the sale of the house."

"Of course that includes a funeral for all six with a six year guarantee. Anything after that will be an additional charge."

Al said, "Well, I won't last six more years, and the military will pay for Vinnie's funeral. Christian's nasty temper will probably put him in jail where he'll be shanked. The state will bury him, but since I pay taxes I'll have paid for that waste of humanity as well." He found that funny and laughed. "I'm not sure how long Ricky here will last. If he's smart enough to get some therapy, he may make it to a ripe old age. If not, who knows? At any rate, he has a work ethic and can pay for his own funeral. Here's my personal check for the full amount. Tony Marino, the bank president will okay it."

The funeral director handed Al a form to complete that listed the names of the family, which he signed and returned. Horace checked it over to see that his name was listed as Horace and not Ricky or Rick because he hated those demeaning nicknames. His mother had named him Horace and Horace he would be until he died. The director said, "Have you decided on what church Mrs. Tedesco will be buried from?"

"We've chosen St Catherine's."

Horace asked to see the funeral home online obituary because he wanted to make sure that his friends from the city had the information. He looked up in confusion. "Why does this obituary list a Kelly Christine Thompson Hogan of 22nd Street, New York City as a daughter-in-law?"

The funeral director explained hesitantly. "This was phoned in by a man earlier today. It's here and in the newspaper. I doubt the paper can change it at this late date, but we certainly can."

Horace was annoyed. "Never mind. We have to go to the restaurant and order the food."

At Al's favorite Italian restaurant the hostess handed them a menu for the various funeral luncheons.

"The $24.95 special is our most popular because it has the widest variety of choices, and while some people prefer spaghetti, others feel it is just too messy to eat, especially if any children are coming; so they prefer the ziti."

She explained the dessert offerings. "Most people prefer the tiramisu, but we have sorbet for those that are lactose intolerant. Sodas are included; is wine required?"

Al thought about Christian, who was off with his drinking buddies. "No liquor of any kind, people will be driving, and I refuse to be responsible for any accidents. We'll stick to soda."

The hostess asked, "How many people do you expect?"

Al turned to Horace. "Your mother wasn't well liked, so not very many."

A livid Horace pulled Al aside. "Mom had lots of friends."

Al challenged him. "Name one."

Two names immediately popped into Horace's head, "Eugenia will be here and her daughter. Eugenia won't come alone to a funeral."

Al explained, "Eugenia was your mother's hairdresser and I'm paying her to do your mother's hair before the viewing. That's two. Who else?"

Horace knew his aunt was close to his mother, "Aunt Pegeen and her family."

Al shook his head. They live in Rhode Island and haven't seen each other since your mother called her daughter a whore for wearing a short skirt at Easter Mass. No love lost there."

"Kasey, Georgia and Val will surely come."

Al responded in disgust at his son's obtuseness where his mother was concerned. It explained why he never had successful relationships with women. "If I was you, I wouldn't bet on it."

Horace was bereft, "Don't you think anyone will attend?"

Al turned to the hostess, "I'll get you an exact count later today. Here's my credit card as a guarantee for ten. I'll give you twelve hours notice if we expect more."

143

They headed home in silence. Al found himself looking at his middle son in a different light and hoped he could patch things up before he headed for the mausoleum himself.

As Horace closed the door to Al's guest room, he realized he needed the Shultze-Hogan family in his life. He thought for a very long time. He was finally able to admit that his fears were holding him back from succeeding in life. He resolved to take Georgia's advice and find a good therapist after getting a job for Christian. He knew his father was wrong about the number of people to expect. His mother always said she couldn't spend more time with him because she had so much volunteer work to do with her friends. He was certain that tomorrow would prove him right. His mother wouldn't lie to him; he was as sure of that as he was of Emma's love.

Horace discovered, to his dismay, that Al was right; there were only ten people at the funeral. Georgia and Kasey didn't come, but he was pleased to see Val, who said she was "representing the family." Al made sure she sat next to Horace, whom she hugged with fondness. She handed him a card, which he assumed came from Georgia or Kasey. But when he opened it, and a $5.00 bill fell out, he realized Nick must have sent it. He remembered trying to cheer the boy at the airport by pulling $5.00 from behind his ear. Tears started to well in his eyes because he missed Nick who loved calling him Rick.

Al read the printed card aloud, "To the Tedesco family. I wish I could be there to see Rick. My thoughts are with you. Please use the money to honor your mother. Love, Nick." Al was impressed. "Nice kid, how old?"

Val told him, "He's eight, and adorable. We all love him to death."

Horace wept as he re-read the card, but managed to pull himself together. He squeezed Val's hand. "I really appreciate your coming."

"I'm really here for all of us, but there are many and varied reasons for the absence of the others."

He nodded in understanding and told her, "I'm heading to Virginia to for a few days to find Christian a job. He needs to gain some self-respect and, hopefully, being away from here may just make him into a man."

Al looked at Val, who rolled her eyes. Al, who never understood his son's denseness where Christian was concerned, said, "We all agree with that."

Chapter 24

The Letter

Horace took the train to Washington, DC where he once lived. He knew Bill Bernard, the manager of the Marriott in Crystal City, a suburb of Washington. Horace played on Bill's sympathies, "Bill, our mother has just died and Christian needs to move to a different part of the country." In desperation he lied, "They were very close and it is upsetting for him to live at home with her not there."

Bill understood. "Normally, I'd do a reference check, but as you're an acquaintance I trust, I'll give your brother a try. But I can only promise work from Thanksgiving until New Year's Eve. We don't know if business will pick up in 2002. I can provide him with a room in the wing that's under renovation."

Horace shook Bill's hand. As he started to leave Bill stopped him and asked, "Say, your brother isn't married or has a girlfriend who can cover the front desk during the same time period do you? Joyce is out on maternity leave for a month and we're short staffed."

"No, Christian doesn't know many women. I'll ask around where I teach. Aren't there any college students available?"

"We advertised all over but that's when term papers and finals happen. Maybe your brother can think of someone

146

to keep him company. Get him down here as soon as you can."

Horace headed back to New York, phoning Christian on the way. "It's only about a month, but includes a room in the hotel, and I know that your outgoing personality will make you a strong candidate for year-round employment." The phone was on speaker and he heard his Dad humph as Christian left the room yelling, "Dat las waitin' job almost got me killed, jackass."

Al congratulated him, "Good job son. That's the last thing you need to do for your brother. Turns out your mother had a $2,000 life insurance policy attached to her ATM card. You need to sign a few papers, but you and Christian will share the policy equally. If he can't keep this job he'll have a few dollars of his own so you won't need to send him any more money. It's time to focus on yourself."

Horace cut the connection feeling pleased that someone in his family finally appreciated his efforts, even if it was his father. He headed for New York after stopping at the bank in New Jersey to get his ATM card and sign the paperwork.

When he arrived in New York, he found the house in an uproar. Kasey was crying hysterically, "He knows where I am. Barry's found me. What am I going to do? I have to get out of here." She kept saying the same thing over and over and re-reading a letter that was obviously the cause of the problem. Horace was confused. Why was she in absolute terror of this man named Barry? Who was he and what had he done to her? In typical self-absorbed fashion, he had forgotten everything she said about her stepbrother.

Georgia, A New York Story

Georgia turned to him with suspicion, "Did you have anything to do with this? It mentions New Jersey and the timing is very convenient, don't you think?" He took the letter and read it.

Dear Kelly:

He was confused and wondered, who is Kelly and why is Georgia so angry with me? He read on. *I know you are no longer in New Jersey. But you are in New York. I am single, with no kids but I want you to have mine. I am lonely and frustrated and looking for a mate and I want that to be you.*

A perplexed Horace looked up in mystified silence, thinking, I wonder with whom she is involved? When and where did they meet? He concluded it was someone from her school. He continued to read. *Every time I see you I get hard. I yearn for your soft wetness.*

Horace looked at her and tried to conceal his uncontrollable shaking. He continued reading in fascination. *I love your body and know you will love mine, for it is made to satisfy every part of you.*

Horace tried to stop his mind from visualizing the images by questioning, "Who would send a letter like this?" He was filled with a mixture of curiosity and revulsion as he read on. *I do not know if you have a man or not but if you do, you won't want to be with him anymore after I get through with you. I'll have you screaming my name for more.*

Although Horace was scandalized he kept re-reading the letter. He grew more intrigued the longer he read. Georgia, furious at his insensitivity, grabbed the letter. "What do you know about this?"

148

"Nothing. Why would you think I would write such a thing to anyone let alone to Kasey? I love her." He caught himself. "The way I love you, and Val and Nick.

Georgia said, "How can you profess to love any of us when you don't even love yourself? You don't know anything about the subject."

Val remembered the obituary. "The funeral! Her name was listed in the obituary as Kelly Christine Thompson Hogan of New York City."

Horace asked, "Was this letter in a stamped envelope?"

Val said, "Of course it was. Why do you think she keeps saying the name 'Barry'? It's postmarked from Wilmington, Delaware, which is where she lived before she came here."

"But who is Barry? Where did she meet anyone as low-life as this?" asked Horace.

Kasey cried at his thick headedness, "I told you about him. Didn't you even care enough to remember?"

He was confused; he didn't know anyone named Barry. Why were they blaming him? Georgia gave him her harshest look and said, "I'm taking the letter to the FBI in case there are any fingerprints that can be lifted. This is a Federal offense. Horace, you need to focus. Can't you think of somewhere she can stay?"

He pondered a moment and brought forth an idea. "I know!" They looked at him in anticipation. "You can stay with my father."

They stared at him. He was beyond stupid. Val hit him on the head with the envelope "How brainless are you? Think about it. The letter makes it obvious the guy knew she was in New Jersey. He got the name from your mom's obituary at the funeral parlor. She cannot stay with your Dad."

Horace wasn't angry at the insults. They were right; he was brainless. He concentrated. Suddenly he got an idea. "I have the perfect place. The manager at the Crystal City Marriott said they needed a female to cover someone who is out on maternity leave. You could work at the hotel; they have guards on duty 24/7, and you could have your own room in the area they are refurbishing. No one will expect you down there. I'll be coming down to see Christian on Thanksgiving Day, but I can stay longer to watch out for you."

The three women looked at him and then at each other. None of them liked Christian, but if Horace was going to be there for most of Thanksgiving, it would give Kasey time to meet some of her coworkers and get settled in.

Georgia said, "It might just work until we get to the bottom of this. We'll notify the police and put a timer on the lights in Kasey's window. Meanwhile, Val can set up her camera facing the park to see if anyone is watching."

It was a viable idea. Kasey went upstairs to pack. Horace was overjoyed that he had come up with an idea to help Kasey out of her predicament. Things were looking up.

Chapter 25

No Way To Stop It

It was 8:00 P.M., the Wednesday night before Thanksgiving and the end of Kasey's first shift. The manager was pleased with her customer relation skills and especially impressed by how she handled nearly out of control children. The guards on duty, Smitty and Jonesy, enjoyed her bubbly personality and told her she should move down to Virginia permanently, for she had southern graciousness and charm. These former Marines put her at ease and made her feel safe.

Smitty, the taller of the two security guards, handed her a slip of paper with his cell phone number. Jonesy asked for her cell phone and programmed speed dial for both their numbers. "We've never had any trouble with our employees because Bill won't hire anyone unless they come with excellent recommendations. We have a Secret Service mentality here, ever since 9/11. The Pentagon was only a few stops away, and that sure was a scary time."

Kasey agreed, "I was in New York and some things you just can't forget."

Jonesy said, "My folks talk about the Kennedy assassination the same way their parents talk about Pearl Harbor. Some days just stay in your head."

They nodded, remembering the various stories told by their relatives about those historic occasions. Checking his watch, Jonesy told her, "We're off on our rounds, but be sure and call us if you need anything, and Happy Thanksgiving."

"Same to you." Kelly took her room key card and headed upstairs, thinking the term "Southern hospitality" sure applied to those two.

She reached her room grateful that it was Christian's night off and she didn't have to see him until tomorrow. All the waiters worked a double on Thanksgiving because people from the area ate at the Marriott.

Kasey prepared to take a bubble bath. As she turned on the water in the tub there was a knock at the door. She turned off the tap and called out, "Who's there?" Since she didn't hear an answer, she put her cell phone in the pocket of her terrycloth robe and moved to the door calling again, "Who's there?" She was relieved to hear a familiar voice call out, "It's me, Horace." She was surprised and thought he must have gotten an earlier train.

She opened the door buoyantly saying, "Happy early Thanksgiving." On the other side was a drunken, leering, Christian. She gasped as he forced his way into the room, slamming the door behind him and spewing forth words she has heard before, but this time they were not from Barry.

"It's present time fur two." He laughed as he ripped off her robe. She screamed and fought, but was helpless against his brute strength. Spying her cell phone under the bed, she grabbed it and pressed 1 screaming, "Help, someone, stop, Barry, please stop!!! Christian, no, please no, Barry no!!!"

She was flipped onto her back, and cut by a gold insignia ring as her attacker smashed her across the face.

Kasey screamed, "Christian!!!" and blacked out. At last Christian was able to achieve what he came to do. Smitty and Jonesy broke into the room. Smitty cursed him and with one move knocked him out, threw him over his shoulder, and took him away. Jonesy gently covered the terrified girl with her robe and a blanket. She was shaking uncontrollably and crying. He held her in a fatherly fashion as she blurted out through her gasps, "He pretended he was his brother. I didn't let him in on purpose. He forced his way into my room and he, he, raped me." She shivered uncontrollably.

Jonesy wanted to call 911 and report the incident, but Kasey refused, "No, my name will be all over the papers and my stepbrother will find and kill me. No, not the papers."

Jonesy tried to reassure her, "Miss Kasey, the paper cannot release your name. You're a victim."

"No, I don't want anyone to know. Please. I can't press charges."

"All right, but that scum won't be employed here after I tell Bill what happened. It's assault and battery at the least; you've got a cut on your face from his insignia ring. I'll get you a first-aid kit. That guy should be locked up."

Jonesy didn't like leaving her alone, but he needed to make his rounds. "You stay in the room and only open the door to Smitty or me. We'll call first so you know it's us at the door."

She locked the door behind him and placed a chair under the doorknob. It was just like the incident with Barry. She continued shaking, and tried to warm herself in bed. After Jonesy brought a first aid kit, she relocked the door, and moved to the tub to wash off the filth. Even though she knew that two ex-Marines had her back, she stayed awake all night.

The next morning there was a knock on the door. She heard a voice that sounded like Horace. She began shaking, "No, please god, no, not again." She speed dialed and the Jonesy and Smitty picked up a man outside her door holding a bouquet of flowers. "It's us; there's a guy here named Horace who says he knows you. Should we throw him out?"

Kasey opened the door and Horace gasped, "What happened to your face?"

She replied in anger, "Your mother's favorite son beat me and raped me last night."

Horace was stunned. "I cannot believe he would do such a thing."

Smitty shook him as Jonesy yelled in his face, "You better believe it buddy. We tried to convince her to press charges, but she wouldn't."

Horace was in denial. "There must be a mistake, Christian could not do anything like that. Are you sure it really happened?"

Jonesy said, "Listen, moron, why do you think she's wearing a bandage? Your brother backhanded her with an insignia ring. I saw the impression under the bandage. Miss Kasey, we should toss this jerk out too."

Smitty agreed. "Definitely. He's probably as rotten as his brother. There's a family sickness if you ask me. The sooner you're rid of him the better."

Kasey shook her head. "No, I'm afraid to be alone.

Horace attempting to gain their respect said, "I saved her life on 9/11." The two looked at each other with skepticism and then at this skinny man who stood before them. Smitty looked wary. "OK, if you say so, but dial us if he gives you any trouble." They left.

Horace's cell phone rang constantly until he finally shut it off. Every time it rang Kasey started shaking and crying. His heart went out to her and he said, "Why don't you get some rest? I promise that I will sit by the door and be right here to protect you. We will talk when you wake up. Please, Kasey, I know this has been traumatic for you. You need to sleep. I promise I won't leave. I'll be right here."

He made her feel safe. He was exasperatingly asinine about things, but he cared and she was overcome with exhaustion. She pulled the covers over her head, lay in the fetal position and fell asleep as Horace sat and deliberated.

A few hours later, she woke and saw him pondering in the chair by the door. She felt better. Occasionally he inspired confidence. He said, "Kasey I've been thinking and I need you to hear me out!" She looked at him. "I know Christian hurt you by backhanding you and that you blacked out. I believe that and I don't know why he would do such a thing except that he was drunk. I know that isn't an excuse, but I want you to think about everything that went on. The only reason I suggest this is because I learned in my psychology class that sometimes situations that haven't been

155

dealt with can seem to recur even though they don't."

She looked at him with horror in her eyes. "You think it didn't happen?"

"No, I'm saying that when you blacked out, the incident with Barry came to the forefront of your mind. The important thing for you is to be sure that it wasn't a flashback. Until you confront Barry, you will never know. You will never be able to heal from the horror of what Barry did and possibly never be able to have a strong physical and healthy relationship with a man. You want that, don't you?"

Kasey nodded. He continued, "You want children don't you?"

Kasey nodded again, she loved children of all ages.

He persisted with his idea, "Then you must confront your stepbrother, Barry."

Kasey shuddered at the name. "I can't."

"I think you are strong enough to face him." His chest swelled with self-importance as he urged, "I am certain that you can face him if I am with you." He glowed with over confidence.

She looked at him hoping that he could end her nightmare, "You will go with me?"

He felt heroic. "Of course, I could never let you go into that type of situation alone. I'm your knight in shining armor. Remember me, Ricky?"

She smiled faintly, knowing how much he hated the name and asked, "Tell me, what do you know about confrontation? I think we should call and get Georgia's opinion on this."

He felt himself becoming jealous that she would turn to Georgia rather than him. He said, "Well, I did get an A in my psychology class; besides we can't talk to Georgia about this because you think it is my brother and she hates him."

He pursued his goal of making her rely on him in order to raise his own self-esteem. He said, "All the girls that told me stories of their abuse felt empowered after they confronted their attacker."

Focused on puffing up his importance, he neglected to tell her he only heard two stories from girls in his psychology class and was so embarrassed by the subject matter that he tuned them out. He also missed the session when the instructor broke the students into teams where the abused wrote out the objectives for the confrontation. Thus, Horace didn't realize the necessity of rehearsing the objective of the confrontation, the advantage of role-play, and the rule that the confrontation must take place in a neutral space, never in the abuser's territory. Those were all important factors that Georgia, as one trained in psychology, would have counseled Kasey to do.

Later in the day, Horace rented a car and drove a terrified Kasey to Pennsylvania. He had called ahead and pretended to have some inheritance money for Annie Thompson Reilly. Barry assured him that he could take the check as next of kin. Horace was in a smug mood. He had tricked Barry and he wasn't used to bettering many people.

As he drove down the Baltimore Pike he remembered the first night he and Val saw Kasey standing in the rain. He was so self-absorbed in his thoughts that he never noticed that Kasey was uncommunicative throughout the two-hour drive. She meekly pointed to a driveway and he turned in. The two-story house was shabby and dilapidated, which surprised him for he thought she came from money.

As he parked the car, the door opened and there stood "Barry, the Bruiser." Kasey quaked in fear and refused to get out of the car. Certain they had made a mistake she pulled her cell phone from her purse to call 911. "Horace, please, let's get out of here. We can't accomplish anything." She choked on her words and slid down in the car seat hoping that Barry wouldn't see her.

Horace felt significant as he stepped from the car. He asked in a pompous and superior tone, "Are you Barry Reilly?"

Barry held out his hand, hoping to see the check he had been mentally spending since the phone call. "Yeah, and you must be d' man from d' bank with the check."

"No, I am not. I am here representing Kasey."

"Who? I don' know a Kasey."

Horace drew himself up to his full height and in an authoritative manner said, "Do not lie to me. She is the stepsister you abused for months. She is here to speak to you about an incident that occurred last summer." When nervous, Horace's speech became overly dignified and stuffy, which pissed Barry off.

"Oh, you mean Kelly, d' whore dat ran off jus when I needed her? Is dat 'er in d' car?" Barry walked over to the car, beat on the window and started yelling, "Hey sweetie, you come back for more of my cum?" He laughed at his crude joke as Kasey slid further onto the floor and hid her face in the seat.

Horace made a fist and reached out to hit Barry who adroitly sidestepped the feeble boxing maneuver, grabbed him in a headlock and used Horace as a lightweight punching bag. A terrified Kasey dialed 911 and gave them the address. She was hysterical and barely able to make herself clear to the woman at the other end of the phone, but she was assured that help was on the way.

Kasey jumped over to the driver's seat and turned on the ignition. She honked the horn as Barry slugged and hurled the unconscious Horace onto the hard rocky ground. He started for the car. Kasey gunned the motor and screamed, "I'm going to kill you." She started toward him just as she heard police sirens in the distance. Barry leapt out of her way, missing death by inches. She slammed on the brakes as a patrol car skidded to a stop in the gravel driveway.

Officer Murphy put the handcuffs on Barry without asking any questions. Kasey, seeing that Barry was restrained, rushed over to Horace who was coming around and in obvious pain. Officer Gallagher, a female officer asked, "What's the problem Miss? Did he attack you?" Kasey shook her head and began to cry, "Not this time but he beat Horace quite badly."

Officer Gallagher confided to her partner. "This one is out on parole for drug possession. He served a year, but I think this fight gives us probable cause to search the home, especially his room and see if there are any drugs on the premises."

Murphy said, "I wouldn't mind seeing this troublemaker put away for a long time." He looked at Kasey. "I bet you wouldn't either Miss." He shoved Barry in the back seat of the patrol car while Officer Gallagher left to search the house. "How about your friend here? Does he want to press assault and battery charges?"

Horace, still in pain, pulled himself up and clung to a tree for support. He shook his head no. "I don't think I have time to come back and forth from New York for a trial. I may be moving to Australia soon."

Kasey looked at him in disgust, and for the first time she saw him as the forty-year-old hopeless human being that he was, a man with no understanding of life or people. If Barry had owned a gun, they would both be dead. This was just another example of Horace not thinking through the ramification of his actions.

Officer Gallagher returned with five bags of heroin. "I found these under the mattress, and it looks like enough to put him away for a long time. He won't be bothering you again."

Kasey sighed in relief as Officer Murphy looked at Horace. "He doesn't look in any condition to drive. You may need to get him checked out at the hospital."

Kasey got in the driver's seat. Horace, realizing he was no longer in charge, climbed meekly into the passenger seat. She said harshly as she started for the Wilmington train station, "Don't forget your seat belt." After a few miles of silence, Horace, tried to regain his dignity by saying with confidence, "I do not need a hospital. I am just a little sore. A hotel masseuse can straighten out my back."

She replied sharply, "I don't care anything about you or your needs. You can do whatever you want because I am taking a train back to New York. I have to get away from you and your brother, who you still think did nothing to me but cause a flashback." As they moved closer to the station she expressed her anger at him in crystal clear diction, "The best thing you could do for Christian is to commit him to a psychiatric facility and you should read up on the *fraternal birth order effect*."

"What does that have to do with me?"

"Finally, a question from you! Guess that's one you'll have to research on your own since you didn't pay any attention in your Psych. class." She stepped from the car. "We're here. Good riddance."

She dashed up the steps as the train pulled in. Her timing was great. She jumped aboard, pulled out her cell phone to tell Georgia she was coming home, paid for her ticket, sat back in her seat, smiled peacefully and promptly fell into a deep sleep knowing she was going home to Georgia and safety.

Chapter 26

Something Better Than This

Three hours later, he returned the rental car and called Christian who was living in a run down motel in Arlington. Horace was mentally and physically exhausted. He needed a place to spend the night and entered the sleazy, filthy carpeted room where Christian tried to convince him that Kasey was a whore. Horace, too tired to argue, fell asleep on the couch. Christian shrugged his shoulders and went out to the sports bar to meet some new guys who would buy him drinks.

Late the next afternoon, Horace awakened to his ringing cell phone. He looked at Christian's bed, which had not been slept in all night and wondered why Christian was calling him. Half awake, he answered to discover an enthusiastic Emma in Arlington who wanted to meet him immediately. He leapt from the bed, wrote down the directions and rushed to get his clothes. He winced as he leaned over to open his suitcase. His back was still in pain from Barry's beating. He knelt on the floor to pull out some clean underwear and walked into the filthy bathroom to take a very hot shower.

After dressing and combing his hair, he realized to his horror that he had forgotten his toothbrush. He eyed Christian's dirty, well-worn one and grimaced. He had never used anyone else's but his own. He never even considered borrowing the brush of a girl he slept with. But time was of the essence and he must taste his best for he loved kissing. He crammed the grimy bristles with toothpaste and with distaste brushed away.

Dragging his suitcase to the door, he called a blue top cab in anticipation of meeting this twenty-three-year-old, girl that he had been e-mailing for six months. Fifteen minutes later, the cab dropped him off at the apartment house. After the concierge gained approval and directed him to 5F, Horace knocked on Emma's door in eager anticipation of the four hours of enthusiastic lovemaking she always talked about in her e-mails.

The door opened. Horace was dumbfounded. There stood his future wife. The woman he dreamed about, night and day since June. She was dressed in a shiny red bra and matching thong panties, nothing else. He gasped and gazed in awe at her long black hair, gorgeous smile, tiny breasts and flat hips. He loved everything about her. Her 5'2" height was the perfect size to make him feel superior. She grabbed his suitcase and yanked him through the door. He winced but didn't want her to notice so he just stood there looking. She smiled as she pressed her nearly nude body tightly against his and kissed him long and hard. Horace was surprised that this didn't excite him and assumed it was because his back still hurt from Barry's beating.

She placed his hand on her bare ass and sensually led him to the bed. Even this didn't arouse him. Hoping to curb any curiosity she might have about his performance ability he lied, "I was in a fight last night with a drunk and my back is a bit out of shape. Do you think you could give me a massage before we, er… get to know each other better?"

Emma smiled and wiggled provocatively as she knelt to remove his shoes and socks. She smiled up at him, "Now I remove shirt and you lie down on stomach." He smiled in relief as he lay face down on the bed and she straddled him. He winced at the added weight, but as she massaged his back he felt better and more relaxed. After thirty minutes of kneading and rubbing, Emma yanked him upright and began to kiss him passionately.

Horace was thrilled. He loved kissing. He could be satisfied kissing for more than an hour but Emma was a woman of action and getting very bored.

She knelt to remove his boxers, but Horace stopped her, "I have to explain something to you before we go any further, I…I have atrophied testicles." She was confused by the big words, but she forced the information from him in very broken English.

"What that mean honey?" Embarrassed, he pointed to himself. She got it "Ah, you mean balls." Then she yelled at him with suspicion, "You no good in bed?"

Horace lied quickly, "Not at all, I have had sex with numerous women. It is just that, when I was a teenager I got mumps."

"You have disease? We no have child? I want baby."

" No, no, we can have many babies. I can have an erection, but I …I sometimes need some added testosterone; it helps quite a bit."

She suspiciously watched his skinny, boxer-shorted body run to his suitcase, which he quickly opened. He handed her a tube of cream and asked her to rub some onto his shoulders and upper arms.

"What you need that for? I not want be all greasy, my skin very sensitive."

He gave her some white cotton gloves and assured her, "It will dry quickly."

As she rubbed him with testosterone his slow to react brain wondered, why does Emma use such broken English? He concluded that she was probably frightened.

Impatiently, she asked in a voice that reminded him of Georgia's imitation of her sister-in-law, "How long we wait, honey? I go get hair dryer so you dry quick. I horny for you."

Horace started to worry. He knew from his past failed relationships with women that it would take at least thirty minutes or more of oral enticement for him to be able to satisfy a woman, but he blamed that on the fact that American girls were easily bored and never considerate of him.

The lights were romantically dim as she removed his boxers and said, "You ready, honey, but I know back in pain, so I be on top." She leapt to straddle him and he reached out to her in anticipation. The testosterone was working. Horace shivered in anticipation as she wiggled onto him. It had been so long since he did anything but dream about a girl that being with her brought him to a sudden climax. He sighed in contentment, knowing she was the girl he was going to spend the rest of his life with. He promptly fell asleep, dreaming of a happy, child filled future with Emma as the caring mother of his future sons.

The next morning Emma got a phone call that woke them both. She had returned to their bed after her satisfying threesome with her Brazilian sister and boyfriend in the next room. She responded excitedly, "Yes, I come right away. I get plane to San Francisco and let you know." She pulled one enormous, clothes-filled suitcase from the closet and wheeled it to the door. She grabbed a matching empty one and began packing.

Horace quickly pulled on his boxers, got back in bed and clutched the covers to him, as he said in confusion, "San Francisco. You are supposed to be with me for Christmas in New York. I want you to meet my family since you are the woman I am going to spend the rest of my life with."

She was frenetically ripping clothes from closet hangers. He looked at her in her Victoria Secret underwear and imagined he performed badly. He apologized. "I am so sorry about last night, it will be better, I promise you."

She ignored his begging apology as she flung open drawers containing scanty outfits and a few more subdued ones, which she bought for impressing future in-laws. She threw everything haphazardly into her rapidly filling red suitcase.

Horace was desperate for he saw another dream dissipating before his eyes. Emma, the girl he fantasized over for six months and envisioned carrying on his seed, was running out of his life. He tried to entice her with a guilt trip, something he learned from his Irish mother. "I paid six hundred dollars for two tickets to see *Les Miz*." He wanted her to know that was a lot of money on his salary, which would surely prove his love. "Six hundred dollars is about what my take-home salary is as a research assistant." Anger flashed in her brown eyes. He was perplexed. She screamed at him in a voice that John would liken to Arrawika's fishmonger crudity.

"You no college professor?" She was indignant, and her attitude showed it. She moved toward him, no longer in an undulating sensual way, but in the manner of a woman looking for a fight. Horace pulled the covers up to his neck and slid away as she continued her attack, "I look up salary. Professors make one hundred thousand dollar. More for writing and talking over the world. You lie me."

Horace shook his head. Despite his horror at seeing Emma in this new light, he continued to think of her romantic and insightful e-mails, "No, I would never lie to you." She looked skeptical. He continued, certain that baring his innermost feelings would make a difference, "I love you." She ignored his begging, threw some make-up into her purse, pressed her flat-hipped, nearly bare butt, on top of the overflowing suitcase and zipped it up.

Still wrapped in the covers, Horace continued his attempt to convince her that he had a brilliant future. "For now I am a part time professor. I make three thousand dollars per course and September was my first semester of teaching. One course will lead to another. It will help build my resume and once I get my PhD, my future as a professor will be guaranteed."

"I no care about PhD or resume. I want baby. Mother wants me marry rich man and give her baby. We live good on professor's salary. We buy house in Udon Thani on

Son-in-law Street. Eleven thousand rich Farangs live in Udon Thani and mother, grandmother and entire family get big impress from other women."

Horace, almost in tears, frantically reminded her, hoping the guilt trip, which sometimes worked on American women, would make her stay, "You said you loved me." He appealed to her romantic side, "You loved my writing. You wrote to me about your ideas, your dreams and your passion for me. We shared the same thoughts. I loved your e-mails, your innocence, your honesty, your love of swimming, the way you spoke about marriage and having a family."

Emma raised her second large, red, clothes filled suitcase to stand on its wheels and said triumphantly in her abrasive voice, "I no write e-mails," Horace blinked at her. His stomach knotted. He felt a knife piercing his heart. She threw on a pair of heels and turned to have him zip up her dress, which he did mechanically.

She chortled as she told him, "My Australian professor of English he write." Horace stared. He was appalled that someone had read his personal expressions of love that were meant only for her. She turned to him with pride in her stance and voice. "Teacher give mission. You write sexy e-mails. Get rich foreign man bring his country you get good grade." She patted his shocked face, and cackled with pride. "I sleep with professor and get two Americans, one in New York and one in San Francisco. I get A+. I marry American with most money and best benefits. That not you."

Horace felt like throwing up! His eyes watered. He wanted to cry, but he didn't. It reminded him of his childhood beatings, but Emma was diminishing him with language, not a belt.

She looked at this defeated human with disgust and gave him an order. "You hurry, get dressed and bring my second bag. I need get plane San Francisco. Rich man want marry me. If no like, I go Canada, find other rich man. Easy for Australian citizen get dual citizenship in Canada. If no work out there is always England. Both countries have benefit." She gave him an order as she left the room wheeling one suitcase. "You hurry, I no be late. You bring enough dollar for taxi."

Horace dressed and followed her demands. He closed the door to her cab and watched his evaporated dream of six months disappear in the distance as she smiled brightly and waved goodbye.

Chapter 27

What Kind of Fool Am I?

A defeated Horace rented a car and began the five hour drive north. In his mind's eye he pictured Emma and her teacher, nude, side by side at the computer, alternating between sex and laughter as they wrote romantic responses to his heartfelt e-mails. A sudden pelting rainstorm awakened his sluggish brain to comprehend that the only reason he desired Emma was because he needed a pretty girl on his arm to impress people. He felt shame as he reflected on her scorn at his irrefutable love. As he dwelled on her deception his eyes widened and he gasped aloud in fear. "I didn't wear a condom! I had unprotected sex because Emma wanted to get pregnant and have an American baby."

Too distraught to continue driving he pulled into the last rest stop in Delaware. His overloaded mind returned to Emma and he remembered reading about the sex tours to Thailand and the thought of VD entered his slow to react brain. The words 'syphilis' and 'chlamydia' came to mind. Horace began to sob. He had been made a fool of by a student whore he knew nothing about. He was duped by false e-mails, his own insecurity and an unmitigated fear of facing the possible truth about himself.

As he cried he thought, why didn't I take Georgia's advice? She always said relationships should be based on commonality not just on sex or looks. Horace's mind sped up and he began talking aloud. "Why am I attracted to Asian women? Is it because I watch too much Japanese porn on the Internet? Was Emma just what guys in Chelsea call a 'gateway' relationship?" There were too many unanswered questions for his terrified brain to absorb and he felt like jumping off the Delaware Memorial Bridge.

As the sun shone through the dissipating clouds, he made a snap decision to visit his dad. Horace wasn't scheduled to teach until Tuesday; perhaps he could attempt to create a relationship with this man he despised when he was growing up. He headed for New Jersey, finally admitting that he needed the therapy Georgia always harped about. Now that his mother was dead, he could give up on Christian but he couldn't give up on himself.

Two hours later Horace drove into the driveway and was greeted by a very pleased Al, who waved and shouted, "Hi, Rick, I've leftover turkey if you're hungry." Horace accepted his father's use of the nickname and looked forward to some comfort food. He got out of the car with his suitcase and said, "Do you feel like having company for a few nights? Val and Kasey said we should talk." Al nodded, "They told me the same thing. Come on in." Horace stayed for a week, only going into Manhattan to teach and work. He spent all his free time with Al. As he returned the rental car, he knew that with time and therapy, his relationship with his dad would only grow closer.

Chapter 28

Twelve Days To Christmas

Horace returned to 22nd Street where he found Val and Georgia preparing dinner. They looked at him with anger, but he spoke before they could chastise him. "I'm sorry. I know I messed up, and I will not blame you for throwing me out but please, listen."

Georgia turned off the stove, walked over to him and stood with crossed arms. "Go on." He felt his knees shaking at her cold response but he sped on. "I admit that I need to go to a therapist. My arrogance almost caused Kasey and me to be killed."

Georgia felt he was playing his manipulation card, "Anything else you want to tell me?"

He looked away from her glare of condemnation. "I have problems with relationships and I can finally admit there are questions about my sexuality that I need to explore. Will you please help me?"

She waited until he looked at her. Focusing her eyes on his begging ones, she sighed and nodded. He relaxed as Val said, "It's time to eat. You can have half of mine. It's just cream of tomato soup and grilled cheese sandwiches, nothing Italian." Horace was grateful to be forgiven and sat down in anticipation of some real American comfort food.

Everyone concentrated on completing things before the holidays began. Val received an A on her thesis; Horace's students gave him farewell gifts thanking him for a wonderful semester; and Kasey was accepted at John Jay College in the field of criminal behavior. She had decided to become a lawyer and advocate for battered women.

Horace went to Baruch's main office to turn in his keys. He met the chair of the department who had just gotten off the phone with the dean. "Horace, you're just the person I needed to see." Horace said lightheartedly, "You didn't think I'd forget to turn in my keys did you?"

"No, you did everything very well this semester and I would hire you back anytime."

Horace was excited by the praise. Maybe next semester he would teach two courses, not just one.

"I regret telling you this but due to 9/11, many students have decided to spend spring semester abroad. I was hoping to have you teach two classes next semester, but now I can't offer you even one. I assure you that if enrollment figures rise and I can squeeze in your class I will. At the very least I will give you an excellent recommendation for employment elsewhere. You've been an exceptional teacher and I'm sure that when you get a PhD you'll be able to find a first-rate tenure track job." He shook his hand and Horace walked outside into the cold.

He walked dejectedly to his Wall Street job where a second disappointment awaited. Mr. Flanders informed him that business had dropped since 9/11, and his hours had to be reduced even further. Horace knew this would put a severe strain on his budget since Christian was overspending on their joint ATM Card. He thought, I should have gotten my own ATM card, not kept the joint one Mom's insurance gave us. As soon as I can get to the bank I'll cancel it and get a new one just for me. I am no longer my brother's keeper. He felt relief and thought, hope for Horace, hope for Horace and created a marching melody that raised his spirits.

The marching melody made him feel warmer about himself so he marched to the New York Public Library to see the first floor exhibit. On the way he noticed a sign in a store window that read "Twelve Days To Christmas." He thought, *She Loves Me,* Bock and Harnick. As he walked up the library steps he saw Val taking pictures of children climbing the wreath-decorated lions at the front. She stopped filming. "Hi, Rick, how'd you like to go with me to see the tree at Rockefeller Center?"

He agreed with enthusiasm, for Rockefeller Center boasted not only the world-renowned tree but also a wonderful skating rink, and he enjoyed watching everyone circle around. He offered, "I'll be back with some cocoa while you pack up." She watched his gangly body rush down the steps and noticed that his ears were turning pink from the cold.

He returned and started to sit in front of the lion known as Patience, but she shook her head and pulled him nearer lion Fortitude, saying, "Horace, you are already too patient. You need more fortitude, so we'll sit over here."

He was confused, "What?"

She decided he needed a history lesson, and said, "Mayor LaGuardia named the lions during the Depression to give New Yorkers hope. Don't you think it's appropriate in

174

2001?" He looked perplexed but eventually as he looked at each of the lions he smiled in slow comprehension.

Val opened her backpack and handed him some earmuffs, "Here, your ears are turning as red as my backpack."

He rejected them vehemently, "No, I look silly in earmuffs, they flatten my hair."

She decided not to upset him by commenting, "What hair?" But she knew that after his escalated mess-ups of the past few weeks he needed a strong wake-up call.

She put the earmuffs in her pocket and said, "I need to talk to you and I think you'll take it better coming from me than Mom." He looked at her with chagrin. She continued, "Horace, you always choose the wrong women because you focus on a woman's looks, rather than her intellect and personality. Emma was a perfect example. Once she discovered you had no money, she was off to the next bozo brain. P.T. Barnum and Michael Stewart were right, "There is a Sucker Born Ev'ry Minute." You got roped into an Internet romance without researching the subject or even knowing who was on the other end of those e-mails. For all you knew it could have been a man." Horace sat and half-listened.

Val shook his arm and forced him to focus. She continued, "Men like Uncle Robert and you are like deer in hunting season. They are easy prey for ex-bar girl hostesses, greedy divorcees and schemers who seek them out when they need an escort to a wedding, a free live-in baby sitter or someone to share their expenses. When these women find someone of greater benefit they move on. Too many men fear telling their parents and friends they would rather 'male bond' than live with a woman. So they marry, have children and withdraw into books or TV sports when they realize they have nothing in common with their wife or their kids. Horace, you have always gravitated toward conniving women with their own agendas. They don't care about you, they just use you until someone more suited to their needs comes along."

Horace grew defensive, "What makes you think that you know everything about the topic?"

Val smiled with confidence. "I research a wide-variety of topics, and I read the articles you ignore because your continuing arrogance causes you to believe that you know more about life than anyone else. You are so desperate for acceptance that you never admit that all your female lovers are the same types, greedy and exploitive. You really do need counseling if you are ever going to break this ridiculous pattern that has become your lot in life."

He put his hands over his cold ears and said with resignation, "Perhaps you are right. I wait for people to involve me. I have never been able to take control over my own life. If someone shows any interest in me I am so grateful that I follow their lead like a puppy on a leash." Val nodded and encouraged him to continue. "It explains why I let Christian use me. I am so afraid of losing his love, which really isn't there, that I can't break the cycle.

Val told him, "It's due to your insecurity and the neediness you experienced while growing up. Horace, you tell stories about your fellow workers that you haven't witnessed first hand. You are like a gossiping, lonely old woman who is starved for attention. You need to be honest with yourself or your potential will be stalled forever." She looked at him and held out the earmuffs. He considered how ridiculous he must look with his hands over his ears, and finally able to admit he was stupid for not wearing them, he put them on. Val grinned, thinking that perhaps she had made a slight dent in his avoidance of reality, and they walked to see the tree at Rockefeller Center. Horace was not sure he felt any better after their talk, but Val had given him food for thought and his ears were certainly warmer.

Chapter 29

V. D. Polka

Georgia turned in her grades at the registrar's office. As she started walking, dressed warmly in boots, hat, mittens and a down coat, she thought about John. This was her first Christmas without him. She couldn't bear the thought of buying and decorating a tree. She not only missed John she was upset by the thought of not seeing Nick again.

She stopped at the Moonstruck for a cup of hot tea. She entered, ordered and listlessly paged through their enormous menu. She skimmed the dessert page and her eyes rested on a picture of an oversized, flaky, creamy Napoleon, a dessert John always enjoyed watching her eat. As the waiter returned with the tea, she pointed to the Napoleon and said, "I'll take two, please Juan."

He was confused. "Ees someone else coming?"

"No, it's a family tradition. I'll eat both of them."

When he returned she remembered the last time she had these was with John last Christmas. As she savored the creamy custard on her tongue her eyes filled with tears thinking, no more surprise fun packages marked, To: Georgia; From: Santa Claus. She focused on the next Napoleon and found a bit more comfort in the belief that Rudy, Roberta and John were waiting for her and considered how lucky she was that Val had Kasey as an adopted sister.

178

She was reminded of Kasey's strength in facing Barry, a situation that could have ended in murder.

She finished eating and thought if Kasey can face her abuser I can face my dithering brother in San Francisco. She knew that after one week in California she could wear him down and she could even convince Arrawika that life would be easier without Nick around. She flipped open her cell phone, found Robert's number and hit send.

As Georgia was in the Moonstruck phoning her brother, Horace was sitting in the doctor's office waiting to meet with Dr. Lavine. He had convinced himself that he had a sexual disease for he experienced pain when he urinated. He spent two days on the Internet looking up various STD's and was positive he had 'chlamydia' and probably 'gonorrhea'. He researched 'syphilis' and since he was experiencing muscle pain, a sore throat and a headache, he convinced himself that his increasing hair loss was due to his unprotected one-night-stand.

Dr. Lavine entered and shook his hand. Horace turned away, pulled out a sanitizer wipe and proceeded to clean his hands for it was cold and flu season. Horace was self-conscious when she asked, "What brings you here today?" He had memorized his response from the Internet and sped through the recommended statement, "I'm really embarrassed but I'm worried that I may have an STD or... more than one." He hurried on, afraid he would forget the rest, "I had unprotected sex with...with a...." He blanked and couldn't remember what else he was supposed to say. He blurted out in desperation and fear, "...with a whore I met on the Internet.

Dr. Lavine retained a professional demeanor, handed him a gown and said, "I'll give you time to change and will return with a male nurse to take some blood work and swab you for the lab." A few minutes later she returned with the nurse, who took his blood and proceeded with the painful urethra swabbing. After the nurse left it dawned on Horace that he needed to find out if he was HIV positive. He had finally researched the International sex industry and was panicked. Dr. Lavine returned. Horace looked at his feet and asked in a quivering whisper, "What about AIDS?"

Dr. Lavine looked at Horace's chart. "The weight loss, fatigue and sleeplessness listed on your questionnaire may be stress related. I can test you for HIV, but the results won't be conclusive. You'll need to have more blood work in a few months. I can't tell you not to worry, but I can give you antibiotics to treat any bacterial infections. We'll have to wait for a more conclusive HIV test until well after the New Year. I'm sorry, Horace." She shook his hand and handed him two prescriptions.

Horace went to the men's room to wash up and was relieved to see a sanitizer bottle, which he used over and over until it was empty. He felt very dirty and was extremely worried. Patience used to be one of his virtues, but not in this case. He went to get his prescriptions filled. As he sat at the pharmacy he faced a wall full of condoms and thought, stupid, stupid, idiot! I was a moronic fool.

He walked listlessly home, hiding the prescription bottles in the pocket of his pants. He removed his coat in silence. Kasey hurried by him carrying a package from Duane Reade pharmacy. She tripped over the throw rug at the bottom of the stairs, which caused the package to spill onto the floor. Moving to help her he reached down and realized that the package was a pregnancy kit. He exclaimed in shock, "Why do you need a pregnancy kit?" He shook it at her. "Whom are you sleeping with?"

She hauled off and slapped him. Grabbing the kit back, she screamed in his face, "I'm not sleeping with anyone, you arrogant prick!"

He rubbed his face, but was more aghast at her language than the slap. He slowed down in his condemnation, but looked at her with suspicion, "Then why do you need a pregnancy kit?"

She answered sharply, very close to tears, "Because I should have gotten my period December 12th. It is now the 20th and I am never late. This is your brother's Christmas present to me. Does it make you happy that I am going to have the child of a rapist?"

Horace absorbed the final evidence that she was not lying about his brother. He tried to calm her and in a comforting manner urged, "Let us take the test first. Maybe all the stress made you late; maybe it's something else. Let's be sure."

She no longer felt alone because he was implying that he was there for her. They went upstairs together and he sat outside the bathroom door waiting ten minutes for the results, which she shoved in his face. "There now do you believe me?" She sat on the steps and put her head in her hands crying over and over, "Dear god, what am I going to do?"

Horace tried to refocus her on her Catholic school upbringing, "Kasey, it is God's will." His insensitive imagination was elated that she would be having a child with the Tedesco DNA "You will be a part of my family."

She leapt to her feet and began shaking him so hard he almost fell down the stairs, "You stupid, stupid man. You think this is god's will? You are dumber than I thought. Get away from me." She looked at him in disgust and announced, "I am having an abortion."

He blurted out in shock, "You cannot. It is a mortal sin. Your soul will rot in hell for all eternity."

She looked at him with revulsion and said, "You tell me why."

"Because you are taking a human life."

"You tell me why this a mortal sin any more than killing people in a war? Your older brother Vinnie is fighting in Afghanistan right now. Your father thinks he's a hero and so do you. How is his killing of innocent people and children not a sin? You can't believe one is not a sin while the other is. I am not having your brother's bastard."

He grabbed the stair railing at her use of the word bastard. She repeated, "Yes, bastard. You are a moronic fool if you expect me to carry your brother's baby around for eight more months. I am ridding myself, and the world, of any baby with the Tedesco DNA. Do you understand me?"

He had to admit that what she said made sense. But, if she had the baby, he would be financially responsible for its care. He proposed an idea, "Kasey, we could marry and raise the child together."

182

She listened to his empty-headed ranting. "You always thought I'd be a great father. I was wonderful with Nick; you always said so." He sped on with hope building in his heart. "You and I could raise the child as a tribute to John's memory."

Kasey, who felt sicker the more he babbled on, ran into the bathroom, slammed the door and threw up. He waited, not knowing what to do or say. A few minutes later, she opened the door, "You are an unfeeling, pathetic human being! I should have never confided in you, and believe me, I never will again. I'll talk to Val and Georgia when they come home. One of them will take me to a reputable doctor."

Horace was aghast to see the hate in her eyes. He apologized, "I'm sorry. It is just that my life has so little meaning that I thought your child would give me importance. Please, please, do not tell Georgia or Val. I will accompany you to the doctor and pay the entire cost."

She looked at him with suspicion. "I don't trust you."

"Please, you must believe me. I was insensitive and only thinking of my feelings, not yours. Christian is my brother. What he did to you was wrong, and it is my responsibility to make it right." A skeptical Kasey went to her room to be alone.

Later that night, Georgia returned home to a very quiet household. She had finalized arrangements to go to San Francisco and bought presents for Nick at the Museum of Natural History. She was exhausted, for last minute shopping in New York was always an ordeal, but she felt wonderful about her purchases. As she climbed the stairs, Kasey asked to speak privately. Georgia invited her into her bedroom and closed the door. Georgia said, "You're upset. Tell me what's wrong."

"When we talked at the museum, you said if I was pregnant, you could help. I wasn't then, but I am now. Will you call your doctor to arrange for me to get an abortion under an assumed name? Horace has volunteered to take me and pay for the entire procedure."

Georgia was suspicious, "Horace? He didn't try and convince you not to go through with it?"

"At first he did, but in the end he said it was his responsibility. I may be making a huge mistake, but I want to give him one last chance to redeem himself."

"Do you know what the procedure entails?"

"Yes, I've researched it, and have decided on a MVA, which can be done under a local in the doctor's office. It will only take ten minutes, and after an hour I can come home.

"Are you sure about Horace's ability to pay?

"He apologized and seemed sincere. Do you believe he'll go back on his word?"

Georgia focused on having the girl come up with her own answers. "Kasey you've known him for approximately six months. You've seen him with his brother; you've seen him say one thing and do another. There are times I love him, the way I would a confused son, but most of the time I feel like throttling him. I shouldn't be saying this but although he's made progress I'm not sure he's strong enough able to turn against the beliefs he was raised on for forty years."

Kasey said, "I promised to give him a chance and I guess I'll find out if he is a man of his word." Georgia understood the girl's integrity and agreed to make an appointment with her doctor. She hoped that Horace would not disappoint them again.

Chapter 30

The Money Song

On Friday, Kasey and Horace went to Dr. Lavine's office, which upset Horace. He had forgotten that Georgia and he had the same doctor. Although Horace appeared to focus on what the nurse was saying, he was daydreaming that he was the father of a handsome boy named John Tedesco. It sounded good and he liked it.

The nursed interrupted his thoughts. "Sir, excuse me for repeating, but I need the payment in advance." Horace handed her his ATM card. The nurse said, "I'm sorry but we don't have a machine here that can imprint that. I need your credit card or cash." Horace was embarrassed… "I don't have a credit card. I got in some, er difficulty a few years back, and cancelled it."

The nurse wasn't worried, "There's an ATM machine around the corner. We can wait."

Kasey asked, "How much can you get per day at an ATM machine?"

"Two hundred dollars."

Kasey was angry. "You knew this procedure cost five hundred dollars. You'll have to go to the bank on Ninth Avenue."

Horace looked at the nurse hoping she would say there wasn't time. She smiled and said, "We'll wait. Dr. Lavine is running late today so there won't be a problem."

Horace dreaded facing Dr. Lavine who knew he had sex with a whore and possibly contracted multiple venereal diseases. Now she would think he was responsible for impregnating a nineteen year old and probably insist on testing Kasey for STDs and HIV. In embarrassment he rushed out the door to the bank.

Horace went to a teller with his withdraw slip. "I think this is the correct number."

The teller punched the account numbers into the computer, "I'm sorry sir, there is only fifty dollars in your account."

Horace got huffy, "That is impossible, there was over seven hundred fifty dollars in it last week. Are you sure you punched in the right account number?"

"Oh yes, Horace and Christian Tedesco are listed on the account."

Horace asked, fearful of the answer, "Where and in what amount was the last withdrawal?

The teller pushed a few keys, "Arlington, Virginia. The amount was seven hundred dollars.

Horace felt sick. He returned to the doctor's office, knowing Christian had emptied the entire account. The fifty remaining was required to keep the account opened. He knew Kasey wouldn't believe him. He entered the office and tried to explain. She looked at him with hate, "You planned this. You wanted me to have this baby so you made sure not to have enough cash to pay for the abortion."

He shuddered at the word and covered his ears to shut it out.

She shook him in frustration. "Do you hear what I am saying, Mr. Daydreamer, Mr. No Accountability? I am having an Abortion A-b-o-r-t-i-o-n. And do you want to know what day the child was to be born?" She laughed bitterly. He looked up. "August 22nd. Your birthday."

He was doubly pained.

The nurse asked, "Does this mean you'll be cancelling the appointment?"

Kasey pulled out a wad of money and waved it in Horace's jaw dropped face. "Georgia knew this would happen so she gave me enough to cover all expenses. She even gave me money for a cab to make sure I got home safely." She gave the money to the nurse and said to Horace, "I don't expect you to be here when I am done, and I don't want to see you at home either.

Chapter 31

I Guess I'll Miss the Man

Georgia waited, and considered the last three years Horace had lived with them. He, like Nick, arrived as a frightened child with little self-confidence. Georgia thrived on watching people grow and develop. It only took three short years for her students to absorb her philosophy, relish in her love, gain self-esteem and prepare to enter the world as better human beings. She made little progress with Horace. There were times she found herself overjoyed at each baby step he took, but she wasn't one to exist on tiny forward movement. Her energy and charisma demanded giant steps and her students rarely failed her. But Horace usually did.

The older Horace grew the harder it was to get through to him. It had taken demands on her part to get him to better himself by finishing his degree. Now he was well placed to continue with his PhD and become a college professor. He certainly had the intelligence, but he just didn't have the drive. He gave up too easily. His favorite sport, baseball, required three strikes for an out, but Horace was finished after two. He blamed things on his upbringing but she knew that John, despite growing up in much poorer circumstances, had achieved success and changed his life. John didn't have the advantage, as Horace did, of having New York City in his backyard. There was no chance for Horace without intensive therapy, and some serious changes on his part.

Just then, he walked sheepishly in the door. "Horace, I need to talk to you." He dreaded what was coming. "You know that we do not allow deceitful people to live in our home. You lied to Kasey, and by doing that, you betrayed all of us, including Nick." Horace felt like a child being admonished in front of the entire classroom only no one else was there. Yet, he felt them all around. There was no need to explain about Christian; he knew he never should have trusted him and if he had acted faster and opened his own account this conversation would not be necessary. He understood that his lack of forward movement was no excuse and for once he actually listened.

She said, "You need to pack your things and be out of here by Sunday." Horace began rubbing his head. He felt a shortness of breath and his heart beat more rapidly. She ignored his gasps for air and continued, "I want you to know that over the past three years, I have begun to like you, and I will probably always think of you with fondness, but until you enter therapy and divest yourself *forever* of your brother, you may not live here or be in contact with any of us. No messaging, no e-mails, no phone calls, no contact. I mean it."

The word *like* had given him hope and he lost focus. She once told him that liking someone was more important to a relationship than loving someone. If you loved someone you never *saw* their flaws. If you liked someone you liked them *despite* their flaws. Thus "being in like was more important than being in love."

She continued, "Everyone I know has moved forward with their lives. Devastation, destruction and death are not easy things to live with. You are the only one who has remained in a rut." She looked at him with disappointment. "Today you shamed this family, the way Nick did on my birthday. Do you understand what I am telling you?"

He wanted to run upstairs and hide under the bed, the way he did when he was a child. She repeated, "Do you understand what I am saying?"

Blankness was written all over his face. "Horace, tell me what I just said."

He couldn't.

She grasped his shoulders and forced him to look in her eyes, "Until you begin therapy and divest yourself forever of your brother, you may not live here or be in contact with anyone of us."

Tears welled in his eyes. The woman who adopted him, the only mother who ever cared, was throwing him out. He was a disappointment to himself, to Kasey, Georgia, and Val. Everyone was moving on and passing him by. Knowing he could no longer blame others for his failures, he felt an overwhelming fear of the future. Christian was the crutch he had used for years, but he was too old to change at age forty. He ran upstairs to his room.

Georgia felt like crying in frustration because she failed him. As she considered the last three years he had lived with them, she realized that she hadn't failed him he had failed himself. Of all the people she cared about he was the only one she could not transform, but that was because he did not want to be transformed. He was satisfied with who he was, which was why his future was always going to be one of repeated patterns, parallel paths and roads not taken. Admitting her inability to help him break the cycle, she knew there was nothing more she could do for him. She thought a minute more and realized that she no longer cared. She had wasted enough time, energy, and love on him. Her lack of success with Horace merely strengthened her resolve to give Nick the future he deserved. She went upstairs to pack for California.

Chapter 32

Memory

It was Nick's birthday, December 24th and Georgia was in the house, packed and waiting for the car to take her to Newark when Kasey ran down the stairs. "My prayers have been answered. I just got an e-mail from Mom that Barry has been put away for a long time. 2002 will be a year to look forward to."

Georgia was happy to hear the news and suggested, "Why don't you invite your mother and stepfather for Christmas in New York. They can have my room." Kasey smiled in appreciation and walked her to the curb.

Val, who was filming in the park, saw the airport car and walked over. This was the first time Georgia had flown since John's death, and she was flying from Newark to San Francisco. Georgia kissed her goodbye, and Val wished her a safe journey. "Good luck. I know you'll come home with Nick. Call when you get there." She watched her mother go and knew she would worry until she heard from her. Seeing Lena entering the park with Al, who was carrying, *A Visit from St. Nicholas*, she turned on her camera and faded in on the annual reading as Kasey returned to the house for her coat.

Horace carried his briefcase and two suitcases to the hall. He saw Kasey by the downstairs closet and reached out to help her on with her coat, which she slipped on without looking at him. She said, "I want you to know that every September 11th at 10:05 A.M. I will light a votive candle of remembrance for you." She turned and walked out the door, leaving him very much alone.

Horace became emotional as he looked around the home he had lived in for the past three years. He knew he would miss this family he was no longer a part of and wondered if he would ever feel the same. Pictures flashed in his memory: cooking with Georgia, shopping with Val, teaching Nick how to throw a knuckleball, the family trip to see *42nd Street*. He remembered how happy he was on his birthday, and all their loving presents. Resigned to a bleak future he picked up his luggage, and walked out the door. He looked back at the house where he had spent the richest three years of his life and fought back tears. He turned the corner thinking, Mom always told me I was nothing and she was right.

Chapter 33

Have Yourself a Merry Little Christmas

It was December 24th, Nick's ninth birthday. Georgia had a carry-on full of dinosaurs and an astrology kit for his ceiling. She exited the departure lounge in San Francisco where her bespectacled brother, who still looked the way he did in high school, said, "Hi." Nick rushed to hug her, and she sang "Happy Birthday" as she handed him the carry-on. He was thrilled that she hadn't forgotten.

Georgia, knowing she had to be nice to Robert, put on her warmest smile and said, "Where's Arrawika? I thought she might come with you."

"Her mother is sick and we just put her and the boys on a plane to Isaan. It's a long ride so she won't be back until after you've gone." Georgia felt like shouting hooray, but didn't. She grinned instead and said, "Well it will be like old times in Wilmington, the two of us decorating the tree. I'll tell Nick stories about those days."

Nick smiled in anticipation of his aunt's stories, but Robert said in his irritatingly plodding voice, "Uh...we don't have a tree."

"What!" She exclaimed. "Nick has to have a tree. Let's get one on the way home."

Robert was sure there were none left, but she persisted. They drove out of the airport heading into town where they passed several empty tree centers. She insisted they keep looking. As they neared the house, Nick spied a small tree in the back of an empty lot. "Look, there's one."

Robert said, "It's too runty."

"Come on. Remember the time you had to hand drill out our tree and we tied in extra branches?" Nick knew a story was coming.

Robert was clueless. "Uhh... I don't remember that."

"Sure you do. You sawed off the branches and took out your Boy Scout hand drill and spent two hours boring four holes in the middle of the tree and then you tied in those extra branches. Mom, in her typical short sleeve pleated blouse, straight skirt, nylons and heels, held the tree while I watched from the sofa. You drilled away. The two of you wired in the branches and set the tree in the red holder. It was a three-hour labor of love. After Mom placed it in the corner and you put the lights on it, I was allowed to help with the ornaments. You stood together admiring your 'artistry' when I discovered the unopened tinsel, hurled a huge handful on the unbalanced tree, and it fell on Mom just as Dad drove in the driveway.

"You stood it back up just as Dad came in the room, flopped on the couch and said 'Best tree we ever had.' I thought Mom was going to kill him."

Robert remembered at last and started his deep throated, hesitant laugh. Nick's eyes grew wide as they put the tree on the roof rack and headed home. Robert dragged out the decorations, and they worked until midnight. Nick flopped on the couch and said "Best tree we ever had." They laughed and headed off to their respective rooms.

Georgia had five days to convince Robert that Nick would be better off in New York with her.

At Christmas breakfast, she noticed Robert was sitting with Nick at the table. Robert was reading a book and Nick was picking at his food. Occasionally, Robert noticed he wasn't eating and said, "Eat." Nick took a bite, and Robert returned to his book.

Forgetting about her intent to be charming, she ripped the book out of her brother's hands and said, "What are you doing?"

"Reading."

"Not while I'm here you aren't. Never, ever at the table. The reason Nick doesn't eat is because the only time you pay him any attention is when you see he isn't eating. So he waits until you order him 'eat' and takes a bite."

Robert said nothing. Nick wondered what was going to happen next. Georgia left the kitchen and returned from her room with a photo album. "When you two are finished eating, I want to show you something."

They moved to the living room, she motioned them to the sofa and sat between them opening Roberta's green photograph album full of pictures of their years growing up in Wilmington. She began in 1945. They were in matching snowsuits, sitting on top of a snow cave, an unusual event for a Delaware winter. She showed them a photo of a happy

Robert at age eleven and an exhausted Roberta at age forty-seven. Mother and son had just completed walking up the 897 steps of the Washington monument. Nick was amazed.

Georgia reminded Robert, "Grandpa Rudy and I took the elevator up and down but Mom stoically walked up because you wanted to. She did everything for you."

Robert turned the pages in silence until he came to one of him in his Eagle Scout uniform.

"I remember this." His speech sped up. "It was at Eisenhower's inauguration January 20, 1953."

"You were to march early in the day, but the parade was so long that you didn't go by until well after dark. The day was freezing cold. Dad and I gave up and watched the entire thing on a black and white TV in the Statler Hotel. But not good old Mom. She waited in her nylons, short plastic boots, lambs wool coat and Mamie Eisenhower style hat. She froze to see her favorite child march in that parade."

She noticed Robert's eyes starting to mist and she continued her pictorial and verbal family photo history for the next four days. She talked herself hoarse, but she kept on in her attempt to wear him down.

December 31st, her departure day arrived. She held up two tickets, one for her and one for Nick. Robert looked at her as she said, "Mom and Dad gave us every chance to succeed. They worked hard to give us every advantage. I saw them both through their aging years, never minding the additional work because I loved them both. You never came to see Mom when she was dying in the hospital for a week. She always asked, "When is Robert coming? When is Robert coming? For seven days and nights she asked me the same question."

Georgia looked at him with tears in her eyes and said, "You never showed up. Val and I saw her through the difficult times in the hospital. We were there for her and you, her absolute favorite, never even had the decency to call."

Robert's eyes began to water under his thick glasses. Georgia continued, "I finally realized why you didn't come. You were ashamed of choices you made in your life. And now, it's time you were honest with yourself because the way you live is affecting the future of your son. I love him and I like him. He belongs with us in New York. Are you going to let him achieve all he can or are you going to let him grow up with a father whose favorite word is eat?"

She put a second scrapbook marked family holidays in front of him. She opened it to a picture of the two of them sitting in front of a Christmas tree. She looked impish. He looked bookish.

Robert looked at his only son and said, "Do you want to live in New York City?" Nick was bursting with pride for his father had finally asked his opinion.

Worrying that he may hurt him, but wanting to spend his life in New York he said, wisely, "Only if you will come and visit me at least four times a year."

Robert agreed, "You can go, but be sure and e-mail." Georgia said, "He'll do better than that, he will phone, every Sunday, right after church."

Robert smiled, knowing how much she was against organized religion.

Georgia opened her cell phone and hit send. A few minutes later there was a knock at the door and Robert opened it to find Annan, his Thai neighbor and licensed California lawyer. Annan entered carrying a legal looking document and a heavy cosmetic case. He said, "Robert, I explained the situation to Arrawika before she left and she signed these legal papers giving Georgia and Val custody of Nick until he is eighteen."

Robert wiped his glasses and returned them to his face as he slowly responded, "I don't understand. How did my sister find you?"

Annan answered, "We were at Syracuse together. I was a pre law/drama major and she focused on musical theatre and directing. We did lots of shows together. She heard I had moved next door to you and asked me to talk to Arrawika. This case is filled with jewelry in the amount of twenty thousand dollars. Arrawika has agreed to stay out of Nick's life in exchange for the jewelry she picked out before she left. It's all legal, but not until you sign it as well.

Robert finished reading the document. He saw the determined look on his sister's face and knew that Arrawika never would let him have any peace if she didn't get the jewelry. He signed. Annan shook his hand and said, "I'll file this with the court and send you a copy."

After a hug with Georgia, he exited, saying, "Have a Happy New Year." Robert took the jewelry and started to return the photo albums. Georgia said, "No keep them. We'll be sending you lots of pictures of Nick you can insert. It will remind you that he is being raised the way we were and you will know that attention is being paid to him on a daily basis."

Robert picked up her suitcase and said ploddingly, "What about his clothes."

Georgia took Nick's hand and said, "We'll have fun scouring the city thrift shops."

They headed for the airport and Nick knew that he was going home.

Chapter 34

Come Back to Me

Val and Kasey had decorated a tree so Nick could enjoy it until January 6th. They waited for him at the house knowing he wouldn't arrive until after midnight. It was New Year's Eve and they watched the Times Square madness on TV. As the ball descended an exhausted Georgia entered, followed by an excited Nick who looked at the tree and said, "Best tree we ever had." Val, knowing to what he referred, laughed, picked him up in her arms and carried him to his room with Kasey following.

Georgia turned out the lights, smiled at the tree and thought of John. Needing to talk to him she went to their room and studied the patchwork memorial quilt square that hung behind her favorite picture of him on the Jet Ski. She smiled and said, "He's home and I couldn't have done it without you. "

The next morning, long after breakfast, Nick wandered downstairs looking for Rick. He was upset to learn that his buddy had left and probably wouldn't be returning. The lights on the tree twinkled brightly and bounced off the fragments of outside light shining through the stained glass windows. There was a knock on the door. Georgia answered to greet Lena and Al. Georgia introduced Nick, who noticed the dark-haired resemblance, and asked about Horace. Al told them, "He's living in New Jersey with me. We talk a lot, trying to make up for all those lost years. Christian called several times from Virginia, but Rick refused to talk to him. Last we heard, Christian was jailed for assault, battery and armed robbery. He's going to be put away for a long time and none of us will miss him." Lena pulled his arm and the two headed for the diner.

Val thought, way to go Ricky, one giant step for you. They bundled up and headed uptown to the tree at Rockefeller Center. The place would be crowded with tourists, but it was a great way to start the New Year. As they passed St. Patrick's, Georgia said, "I need to light a candle for Rudy. Meet me by the fountain. I'll call if I can't find you."

She entered the crowded cathedral, quickly dipped her hand in holy water and made a hasty sign of the cross. She moved to the interior altar dedicated to Saint Anthony, the finder of lost things, knelt to light a candle, and prayed to her father, "Please help me give Nick the life that you and Mom gave us and don't bring me up to your musical theatre heaven until I've accomplished it." She wiped a tear from her eye and attempted to push through a crowd of French tourists blocking the exit. She said, "Si vous plait." But no one moved until a man, holding a beret said in Japanese, "Dozo, onega shimasu. Watashi ni shita ga te kudasai." Gratefully she let him take her gloved hand and followed him as he pushed his way through the crowd. As they exited the church she gave a formal bow of thanks. "Domo arigato gozaimashita." Thinking it strange there was no response from this Japanese tourist, she looked up. It was Horace! They stared at each other, each overwhelmed with emotion but not saying a word.

When Horace found the courage to speak, he looked into her suspicious eyes and stammered, "I want you to know that I have taken your advice, and scheduled counseling sessions that being next week." She stared in stony silence while he continued, "I have been waiting since 6:00 A.M. praying that you would come.

She knew he was playing on her emotions during this season of forgiveness and although Val would welcome the challenge of changing him she had no time to spend on his arrested potential. She had to focus on Nick. Her young nephew needed her and loved her. Horace did not. She started to pull away, but he tightened his clasp on her hand, and led her outside into the brisk air and the sound of chiming church bells. His eyes began to mist, which touched her, and she felt herself weaken, but managed to pull away from him. Her eyes were cold because she didn't want to put up with any more of his lying neediness. She thought if she gave him stringent guidelines that he would leave on his own. She said with firmness, "Since your brother is out of your life by default, I have additional demands." He waited with a mixture of hope and trepidation. She held up one finger, "One, you have to complete your PhD in three years. He nodded. She held up a second finger and stated firmly, "And, no more foreign entanglements." He nodded again. "And finally," she held up three fingers and gave him 'the look'. Horace rubbed his head. Expecting the worst, he choked in a panic, gasped for air and lowered his face. She placed her gloved hand firmly under his chin, but felt herself melting at his little boy neediness. She forced him to look at her and sighed with kind-hearted warmth, "You *must* learn more musicals." Shaking with relief, he embraced her to him, but made sure to avert his face so she wouldn't see his happiness pouring onto the collar of her coat.

After a few seconds, he recovered, stepped back, smiled with pride and donned his newly purchased black beret. She eyed him carefully, reached up, tilted it to one side, admired her achievement as she said, "Now you do look quite debonair."

As they walked arm in arm down the crowded steps, she asked, "Do you have that Tom Seaver baseball card with you?" He opened his wallet and showed it to her. She said, "A young boy named Nick is waiting with Val and Kasey at the fountain." Horace gave an enormous yelp, flew down the steps, charged across Fifth Avenue and faded into the crowd. As usual, he had forgotten all about her. Knowing that Val's patience and fortitude were better suited to making a difference in Horace's future, a relieved Georgia crossed Fifth Avenue humming "I am Free." She entered the New Year invigorated by the idea of 'opening new windows' for her nephew, Nick.

Epilogue

Mom finished her novel in a record four months. She went into her hyper-focus, obsessive-compulsive mode and worked ten hours a day. It went from 40,000 words to 70,000 and eventually she, and her eclectic family, trimmed it to its current size.

When I asked when she was starting our unique family history she smiled and said, "Remember those tied-in-a-bow, happy ending stories I used to read to you when you were growing up?" Of course I did. She grinned and said, "I'm adding to them so tell all your friends to be ready for *Georgia, A Life Remembered* in October of 2013."

I know that book will span the decades, no doubt starting with the birth of my grandmother in 1903 and my grandfather in 1911. Their eight-year age difference, chance meeting and subsequent inter-faith marriage is a shocking story unto itself.

I remember Mom's stories of growing up in the '50's and her campus leader life on the Syracuse campus in the '60's. If she continues through her performing days in the Far East and her travels with my Grandmother on Pan Am 1 during the heat of the Vietnam War it will make for some very interesting reading. I assume she'll include her first year of college teaching during the Kent State massacre. I dread to think that she'll include her recollections about my birth and I may have to write my own novel to set her memory straight as she talks about the foibles of raising a teen in the '90's.

If you enjoyed *Georgia, A New York Story*, watch for other books in the Georgia series.

Mom insisted that I include the *eclectic family* definition as a reminder that you can choose your relatives and in many cases you will be happier if you do.

The 'eclectic family' is created by choice of the participants rather than DNA. These are people of assorted ages that make an impact on who you are or will be. They enjoy being together and comprise the 'relatives' you choose, based on demonstrated trust and love. This diverse family is one you cherish because they are honest with you when you are at your worst, which will help you become your best.

Val Shultze-Hogan October 7, 2012

Coming in 2013

An excerpt from
Georgia, A Life Remembered

Fancy Forgetting

It was the fabulous '50's and we were one of the few two-car, middle class families in Wilmington, Delaware. Dad had a company car so we never had to schedule our lives around office car-pooling. The family car was a new, practically indestructible, 1956 yellow, four-door automatic shift Buick, with power assisted steering. That was the car Dad used when he gave his favorite child driving lessons. The knuckle biting session lasted less than four hours.

His teaching consisted of terrified comments such as, "Watch out for that person! You never know when they may want to end it all." As we moved to the rural roads his fear escalated, "Get over, there's no shoulder on this road and there may be a tractor lurking up ahead." As we passed the multitude of millionaire estates, he imagined the worst and yelled, "For Pete's sake don't kill any of Mr. duPont's cows."

Dad was a wreck as we travelled the narrow roads on the outskirts of Wilmington and he couldn't stop jamming on his imaginary brake as I maneuvered the curves, often on the wrong side of the road. He only persisted because there were no drivers ed. classes and he felt it his duty to save Mom my hyper-focused obsession on getting a license so I could give up my three-speed Raleigh.

He admitted defeat when I attempted the turn into our holy metal one-car garage that was filled with punctures from my missed aim at my backyard archery target. As we both slammed on our brakes, the car connected with the side of the garage and he gave up. His shaking legs carried him into the house for a much-needed nap; it was his favorite method of coping with life's tribulations and teaching me to drive was an enormous undertaking for him.

Mom took over. She was older by eight years so she was the more experienced driver. In 1927 she used her salary as a high school Latin teacher to buy her first car, an oversized Oldsmobile. Scrapbook pictures show a petite beauty barely tall enough to see out of the front windshield. In the '20's there were few cars on the roads and so she taught herself to drive. Thirty-years later she taught me. Mom's patience, courage and fortitude gained me that coveted license by my 16th birthday.

For the next two years I drove my carless friends to the movies, the local burger hangout, the drive-in, school sporting events and anywhere else we wanted to go. As long as I obeyed Mom's rule that none of my friend's could drive the car but me, I could pretty much use that big Buick whenever I wished. She even let me drive her downtown because I was better at parallel parking than she was. And later, when Wilmington got its first parking garage, I thrilled to feel her nervousness when I sped up the ramps on our weekly trips to the library.

I was liberated, carefree and oblivious until 1959 when I got my first summer job in the mailroom of Atlas Powder Company.

That coveted job paid $1.00 an hour and consisted of the usual, tedious mailroom tasks. I soon developed the "speedy mail sorting game" and cut everyone's delivery time by 25%, which mean we could all sit, and chat for an extra fifteen minutes on our breaks. Everyone opened up about his or her lives, dreams and relationships. I was the only one heading for college so I was naturally curious about these new friends who did not come from the usual "boring" suburbs. I found these greasers, musicians, drinkers and dancers fascinating.

One day one of my co-workers asked if I could drive him to pick up his car at the repair shop. I agreed, "Sure, why not." We reached the parking lot and he gazed in stunned admiration at the bright yellow Buick and said with yearning in his voice, "I've never driven a Buick before, do you mind if I give it a spin." I smiled and thought; why not enrich his life a little? It didn't cost anything to make him a bit happier. He took the keys, re adjusted the seat and off we went.

This twenty-five-year-old was one of these friendly guys who always looked at the person he was talking to. Not a safe thing to do in a car because it was a big distraction. Sure enough, driving up a hill he slammed into the car ahead and the indestructible Buick's hood practically sat in my lap. I shoved him out the driver's side door and slid into the seat saying, "Get out of the car. It's my accident, move over." He protested, but I knew it was back to the 1956 Schwinn two-wheeler if Mom ever knew I had broken her strictest rule.

The cops were called, my parents arrived and with innocence in my eyes I told the policeman "It was my fault." The next day Dad lowered the insurance deductible from $250.00 to $50.00. This formerly carefree seventeen-year-old knew nothing about insurance, but this slightly wiser teen knew not to pull a stunt like that again because I couldn't afford to lose my mother's belief in my blue-eyed honesty. Trust was crucial to the rocky relationship with my ever-suspicious mother.

Twenty-six years later my eighty-two-year-old mother was escaping the Orlando summer heat at our New Hampshire home when the phone rang. My husband had just had an accident. I hung up and said, "Poor John, that's something I've never experienced." Mom fixed her eyes on me and said, "Don't you remember the time you wrecked the Buick?" I looked at her, winced a bit and said, "Weeelll, I guess it's time I told you the truth. I wasn't driving…" She gasped in horror. She stared at me as if facing someone she didn't know. Then she put her hands on her hips, stared at me and said, "I'll never trust you again."

I cried with laughter for several minutes as she looked in disgust. I told her that I had made the right decision at age 17 because it saved her years of anguish. She shook her head at my logic and left the room to call Dad whose response was, "It figures."

Mom died at age 89 and learned to trust and rely on me in the remaining seven years of her life because I kept her spirits up during those painful years that included rehabilitation from two broken hips, the loss of her husband of fifty-eight years, and the arduous visits to a myriad of medical professionals. In the end I knew that her once errant daughter, who she often looked at with confused suspicion, had replaced her only son as her favorite child. Certain things in life are worth fighting for, no matter what the odds are for success. My mother's respect and trust was one of them.

About the Author

Carol Lucha-Burns is an award-winning author, playwright, performer, director, actress, singer and teacher who has been involved in over 200 works of artistic creation. As a Professor Emeritus of Theatre at the University of New Hampshire, she developed programs in Musical Theatre, Educational Theatre, Storytelling and Puppetry. Although much of her work is centered in New England, where she won the *NH Theatre Conference Lifetime Achievement Award* and the *New England Theatre Conference Award for Excellence in Theatre Education*, she has also taught, written, performed and directed in Delaware, Pennsylvania, Utah, New York City, Tokyo, Syracuse and Vietnam.

Georgia, A New York Story draws on her knowledge of human behavior and a strong belief in the ability of people's ability to endure, expand and change, despite any obstacle. Like the eclectic family in her first work of fiction, she believes creativity, honesty, tough love, and humor are the most essential tools of survival.

Her award-winning reference book, **Musical Notes**, is a valuable resource for those with an interest in musical theatre.

"This volume is both broadening and professionally focused. As such it is an essential resource for secondary school, college, university, and public libraries." – *Choice*.

"It would be difficult to imagine a more thorough or more useful guide to mounting a musical production: This volume ensures that the shows will go on." – *The Year's Work in English Studies*

Further Educational Texts:

Storytelling, Story and Involvement Theatre
Education Through Dramatization
Puppets-Made Simple for the Class & Teacher
Acting & Directing for the Musical
Community Oriented Drama Programs
Children's Theatre for Education and Enjoyment
Creative Drama

Carol considers her greatest achievement to be the sheer numbers of audiences and readers she has touched, either through works of her own or through those of her eclectic family.

About Georgia, A New York Story

Georgia, A New York Story is a character-driven novel that takes the reader on a stimulating, suspenseful, journey filled with humor, sadness, friendship and affirmation. Its engaging stories and quirky characters come together to form an arresting emotional mosaic of survival.

Georgia, a sixty-year-old professor of musical theatre and drama therapy, heads a colorful but complicated extended family in New York City during the latter half of 2001. Her Chelsea home is a haven for her ever-growing eclectic family of straight and gay friends, students, and neighbors who come and go at will.

Even-keeled John, Georgia's younger husband, and Val, their twenty-one year old aspiring videographer daughter, support Georgia's need to create a safe space with rules and standards where there is never an abandoned soul.

The newest arrivals to this loving household include: forty-year-old Horace, a hapless writer desperate to gain acceptance from his dysfunctional family and achieve marriage with an unknown foreigner he corresponds with via the Internet; nephew Nick, the eight-year-old son of her imperceptive brother and his deceitful, alcoholic wife; and Kasey, an intelligent, kind-hearted, terrified teenage runaway, whose dark secret threatens to destroy any chance for future happiness.

Musical theatre and New York historical references are sprinkled throughout this breakout novel that covers a variety of themes in serious, humorous and visual ways. The story and its characters are psychologically complex and the author addresses the importance of family systems, therapy and creative expression.

Georgia, a New York Story is the perfect choice for book clubs as the characters are multi-generational. Topics for discussion are unlimited and may include: surviving emotional and physical abuse; co dependency; relationships; enabling; coming out; confronting your attacker, and surviving life with humor and love.

READERS' REVIEWS

"I'm glad I've got Georgia on my mind! What a wonderful book! Touching, sentimental, educational and a page-turner, too! I look forward to the next volume of the Georgia series. Reading this wonderful book will have you laugh, smirk, sigh, cry and then grin. In a world where people move too fast to vest themselves in others, Georgia reminds us that the best medicine and the best life lessons come from the caring hearts of others. Read it! You'll be so glad you did!"
– Susan R. Scannell

Carol Lucha-Burns sends you on a journey through New York with Georgia and allows you to fall in love with her family and friends. She remains true to life, where people are flawed, make poor choices, but ultimately are all still seeking love, and friendship of some kind. I loved that all the titles of the chapters are song titles from Broadway musicals, which kept me intrigued to see how each chapter related to its song title. I also enjoyed that Georgia's age did not define her, she enjoyed life to its fullest. I am hoping that I will be

Georgia when I grow up! Looking forward to reading more about her adventures. —Mary Ellen Zaramba

I truly enjoyed this story! The characters were written wonderfully, and I found myself transplanted right to NYC. Looking forward to reading more about Georgia and her fascinating story!———Jennifer Simpson

"'I'm On A Midnight Train to Georgia', *Georgia, A New York Story* is a great read - full of lovingly drawn characters and the kind of details that draw you into a story - effectively creating its own world. And that world is a joy to visit. There is much discussion these days about how 'the family' is changing - this novel demonstrates and illustrates that more than 'changing' - our new families are expanding - and that - in the case of this book - is a heartwarming evolution! Lucha-Burns writes from a solid understanding of - and compassion for - human nature. Her love for NYC is also evident with many references to specific areas and landmarks. These are the details that serve to ground her story in time and place. As the title of my review suggests - reading *Georgia, A New York Story* makes me want to return to Georgia (in this case Lucha-Burns' heroine) once more - to come home and feel the love again. My fingers are crossed that the writer will gift us with another installment enabling us to stay on the 'midnight train' that is this carefully constructed journey! (btw - someone should really option this novel for a movie!!)." – Peter Landroche

"Carol Lucha-Burns captures the imagination with her story of Georgia, a person everyone would benefit from knowing. Literally every emotion is touched as the reader follows Georgia and her eclectic family through an interesting story placed at an interesting time in our history. Hope this is just the first in a long line of Georgia novels!" – Laurel McMahon

"I enjoyed every page of *Georgia, A New York Story* with its quirky characters, dynamic transitions and heartfelt moments. The novel keeps you captivated with every twist and turn, you are rooting for each character as life in New York molds their lives. A great read! I think it should be made into a movie and I can't wait for Carol Lucha-Burns' next volume." – Tina Noonan

"Settle in for a cover-to-cover read when you pick up this engaging New York story. It is a sprawling saga of Georgia Shultze-Hogan, an active drama therapy teacher and three generations of family, friends and students who live at, and visit her home. The main thrust of this excellent first novel by Carol Lucha-Burns is the intersection of her characters as they struggle to find meaning and fulfillment amidst the vast and sometimes unforgiving island of Manhattan. Each character's tale is distinct: the romantic internet correspondence that leads to an astounding first meeting, a mousey teenager who escapes a life of sexual abuse, and the small wayward boy who finds his true home at Georgia's. And more. How do they survive? With Georgia's love and support and the example of her own journey through life. This is an inspiring story that proves the old adage: 'In the school of life, there is always more to learn.'" – Meg Bieniek

"I really loved this book. Mostly I loved the colorful, vivid characters. Georgia is a woman I would love to be or have as a best friend. She is open, loving, warm and very funny. Her love of life and her faith in people fill me with hope. She even confronts tragedy with an eye still open for the little pleasures in life. Instead of closing off to others in despair and resentment-Georgia makes herself physically and emotionally available to her family members, students and houseguests. New York City comes alive in this book also. What a pleasure to visit the many places-diner, parks and city blocks of my favorite city. Lucha-Burns captures a slice of life in pre and post 9/11 New York City. This book captures the special beauty of this city and its dwellers. Lucha-Burns depicts individuals with interests in culture and the arts who join together to form communities and create families that provide support and opportunity for change and growth. This book made me laugh and made me cry. A must read for everyone in 2013." – Joe Carlucci

It kept me on the edge of my seat and I couldn't wait to turn the page. The characters are fully realized and I really cared about them. I highly recommend this book for anyone who needs to escape to another world. Come join their family and you'll never want to leave." —Chuck Bouchard